LigHT WEAVER

><><><><

Books by Thomas Locke

9609

THE SPECTRUM CHRONICLES

LIGHT WEAVER

THOMAS LOCKE

BETHANY HOUSE PUBLISHERS
MINNEAPOLIS, MINNESOTA 55438

Cover illustration by Joe Nordstrom

Published by Bethany House Publishers
A Ministry of Bethany Fellowship, Inc.
11300 Hampshire Avenue South
Minneapolis, Minnesota 55438

Printed in the United States of America

Library of Congress Cataloging-in-Publication Data

Locke, Thomas.
    Light Weaver / Thomas Locke.
        p.   cm. — (The Spectrum chronicles)
    Summary: After an accident in a snowstorm, eighteen-year-
old Dan Simmons finds himself in a strange world where he
must save the beautiful maiden Bliss with the help of the Light
Weaver.

    [1. Fantasy.] I. Title. II. Series: Locke, Thomas.
Spectrum chronicles.
PZ7.L7945Li   1994
[Fic]—dc20   94–19919
ISBN 1–55661–432–2 (trade paper)   CIP
                                                           AC

This book is dedicated to

Jean Reversat

A friend of great courage
and great heart.

THOMAS LOCKE is a delightful addition to Bethany's team of writers, and his exceptional creativity has taken flight in this latest book for teens. An avid fantasy and science-fiction reader himself, Thomas Locke offers the young adult audience a thrill-packed tale with a spiritual message that spans both worlds.

Prologue

There was once a land where waterfalls could only rain upon beds of diamonds, and butterflies could not take flight until a beautiful maiden painted their wings. Babies heard the speech of heaven from angels only they could see. And all people everywhere knew the value of a smile.

Then changes came, as changes often do, neither welcome nor wanted, but coming just the same. Because the people had been born to peace and thus valued it less, they let it pass with little grief and less concern. Swept up in the thrill of selfish pursuits, they forgot the reason for which they smiled. Dark forces were granted entry, because none wished to accept the challenge caused by their coming. And this blessed land traveled the vast distance from peace to the very brink of unending chaos.

Thus a knight was needed. A man stalwart and strong, holding steadfast to the eternal ideals. A hero.

Into this land there came a man, from where no one knew, not even himself. He arrived weak and feeble and uncertain, but he did not remain so. He departed a knight, with honors bestowed and praises sung. He was granted a sword whose blade was not of metal but of golden light. He was asked to bear the shield of eternal knowledge. And upon his head was placed a crown of stars.

But how this came to be is a tale of gallantry and heroism and the wisdom of old. It is a tale of adventure and testing and rising from the flames of despair.

– ONE –

Dan flung open the van door and slid inside on legs both wet and numb. He fumbled with the keys, then had to stop and blow on his hands before he could fit the right key into the starter. The motor ground slowly, as cold as he was. "Please," Dan muttered. "Just this once, okay?"

Resentfully the motor grumbled into life. The heater threw out fitful breaths of stale air. The windshield wipers smeared great fat snowflakes into wet streaks across his vision. As far as Dan knew, the van had not been driven since the early summer. When he had been assigned the van three days ago, he had discovered a banana peel in the back, left long enough to have turned black and hard as coal. The van was old and cranky and should have been scrapped long ago. But somebody at the head office had decided it was fine for part-timers working the Christmas rush.

Dan checked his schedule of pickups and deliveries, using a pocket flashlight he had thought to bring along. The van's own inside light had about as much power as a firefly. Even though it was barely past midafternoon, the day was already dimming, gray and sullen. Dan hit his turn signal and checked the flow of traffic as best he could through the steamed-up windows. He gunned the motor and drove off.

Traffic was tense and surly and very heavy. Dan guided the ungainly van through a slushy lane-change, and pushed away the same worry that had been dogging him since he answered the newspaper ad for this job. Nowadays, Christmas was a time to earn money for school. This was the best-paying job he had been able to find, working as courier for a local express delivery firm. The problem was, the job called for more hours than he could give and still have time to prepare for next week's exams.

Dan caught sight of himself in the rearview mirror. His forehead was creased in a frown of concentration and fatigue, an expression he was wearing more and more these days. Life had not been easy since his parents had passed on two years before. Since then, a lot of the strands of security binding his world had unraveled.

Money was constantly tight. His sister traveled almost continually since their parents' accident. She returned home every eight months or so to earn more money, then took off again. Dan traced her movements on a great world atlas, underlining each new location as she wrote her infrequent letters. He spent many lonely hours wondering what it was she saw, hoping to join her once school was over and done. He missed her more than he knew how to say. Dan had already bought her a Christmas present, though it would be more than three months before he could give it to her. Buying the gift somehow brought her closer.

The light up ahead turned red, and the van did a slippery four-wheel skid before stopping. Dan released his fear-grip on the wheel and took a breath. The snow was falling in great clumps, obliterating his view of everything more than twenty feet away. Few of the cars waiting alongside him had been able to stop in a straight line. The street's icy slush was almost as deep as the tire rims. And the snow showed no signs of stopping.

Dan glanced another time into the mirror and mouthed the word that came to mind—average. It was the word used most often to describe him. Hard-working, earnest, polite—and average. Dan had long since decided there was no worse word in the entire English language. Even his friends considered him a little on the boring side.

The light turned green, and Dan started forward. He had to veer sharply as the car beside him spun sideways, unable to get a grip on the icy road. Which meant his eyes were not facing forward, not until the blare of a horn spun him about, just in time to see the great looming shape of a truck careening sideways and out of control, headed straight for him, just enough time to draw in a breath but not to shout his fear before the truck hammered into his van, side to side, lifting him up and carrying him away, into dark oblivion.

The snowy holiday weekend began with a typical rush at the city's main emergency room. Three ambulances arrived at once. Flashing lights. Sirens. Screeching tires. Shouts from the paramedics as they threw open doors and hustled the stretchers into the orderlies' waiting arms. The orderlies then banged and clattered and shouted as they rolled the newcomers into the hospital.

The resident that evening was a doctor by the name of Prain. He was tall and prematurely bald, and what little hair he had left was as gray as his skin, which was as gray as his eyes. He was a fussy man who lived for forms and orderliness and procedure. He wore a crisp white doctor's coat, starched to boardlike stiffness. His face was frozen in a dissatisfied pucker, giving the impression that he had been fed too many lemons as a child.

Dr. Prain made his disgruntled way toward the receiving station and asked, "What was that all about?"

Nurse Stout shared the doctor's dislike for emergency room drama. She was normally a hall nurse, working ER holiday duty because she needed the money. She replied, "A car accident, a house fire, a heart, and a bar brawl."

The doctor sniffed. Tonight was supposed to have been his night off. And he was supposed to have finished his ER stint last month. But the holiday rush had all the residents doing extra duty. "Which one is mine?"

"Take the accident," Nurse Stout answered. "He'll probably be assigned to your ward."

"Bad?"

"Possible broken leg, from the sound of it. Hip too, maybe. And a probable concussion."

"Better give the duty surgeon a call."

"I already did." She pointed off behind her. "Room three."

The ER was not separated into rooms at all, but rather cubicles with curtains. Dr. Prain entered the third cubicle and swept the curtain closed with a practiced jerk. "What's the picture?"

"Man's out cold," the orderly said, not looking up from helping a nurse cut off the young man's trousers. "I mean, we're talking deep freeze here."

"Pulse is steady at sixty-five," the nurse reported. "Temperature normal. Blood pressure stable at one-twenty over seventy."

All normal signs. Dr. Prain inspected his patient. A young male, aged in the late teens or early twenties, in good physical condition. Normal skin tone except for a slight discoloring on his forehead, where he undoubtedly had struck the windshield, and a further plum-colored lump on his upper thigh. "No bleeding?"

"None."

"You checked his scalp?"

"Yes, doctor."

Dr. Prain palpitated the area surrounding the patient's discolored thigh. There was nothing to suggest a severe break. Possibly a hairline fracture, but he doubted that it was anything more. "EKG?"

"All normal."

The doctor pressed on the young man's exposed abdomen. Normal reaction. "No immediate sign of internal bleeding."

"Pupils are not overly dilated," the nurse went on. This was an important indicator for possible drug use. "No alcohol on his breath."

Gingerly the doctor inspected the young man's forehead. No immediate indication of serious fracture. "What shape was the car in?"

"Mangled," the orderly reported with glee. "Medic said they had to wait for the firemen to cut him out through the roof."

"The patient was unconscious throughout?"

"Slept through the whole thing," the orderly replied. "Way I'd like to do it if that ever happened to me."

The doctor inspected the patient's eyes for himself. Normal reaction to light, nothing out of the ordinary. He listened to the heart's steady lub-dub, the calm breathing, and found himself utterly baffled. Why didn't the patient wake up?

"Name?" Dr. Prain snapped. He loathed mysteries of all kinds. Mysteries indicated a lack of knowledge and order. Dr. Prain lived for a structured, orderly world where all was known and everything had its proper place.

"Driver's license and student's ID for Dan Simmons," the orderly read from the young man's wallet.

A young child began wailing in the next cubicle, and Dr. Prain stiffened. This was what he hated about ER. Everything about it shouted disorder.

"Go find the surgeon," he said crossly. "Tell him if there's anyone else waiting treatment, he should see to them first. This young man does not appear to be in any immediate danger. Get him up to X-ray. Head, spine, legs, abdomen, the works."

Just as the gurney was being wheeled off, the young man moaned a single word.

"Bliss?" The doctor stared at the patient. "Is that what he said?"

"Sure sounded like bliss to me." The orderly grinned and pushed the gurney from the cubicle. "Like I said, the man is way out. We're talking beyond ozone. Interplanetary orbit all his own."

Dr. Prain watched the young man being wheeled away, and wondered at his own reaction. He did not think the leg was broken, and there were few initial signs of serious concussion. In all likelihood, the young man would soon wake up with a splitting headache and a sore leg, and be allowed to go home.

Yet there was something about this patient that he did not like. Not at all.

Another shout from the front doors spun him around. Dr. Prain gave an exasperated sigh, pushed the young patient from his mind, and turned to face the next onslaught.

–Two–

"Are you all right?"

Dan struggled up off his back. Every muscle from his toenails to his hair follicles complained. He let out a long groan.

"You fell very hard," a sympathetic voice said from behind him.

He managed to make it into a seated position. Gingerly he swiveled around, recognizing nothing that he saw. Inch by inch he turned until he could see who was talking to him.

It was a very small llama. White. "Did you hurt your head?" the llama asked.

Dan took another look around. He saw green in every direction. "Where am I?"

It was the llama's turn to look confused. "Why, here, of course. Where else?"

Dan turned back to the llama. It was only about two feet tall but had the sturdy stance of a full-grown animal. "Where's the van?"

The llama cocked its head to one side. Great limpid eyes inspected him with gentle curiosity. "The what?"

Dan gave the vista another glance. It remained as confusing as before. He was seated on a broad hillock looking out over green fields as neat as a manicured lawn. The distant groves of woodland appeared to be planted according to someone's master plan.

He shook his head. The last thing he remembered was driving slowly through the hardest snowstorm he had ever seen, when suddenly a truck had appeared out of nowhere, careening directly for his side of the van.

And now he was here.

He turned back to the llama and asked shakily, "Am I dead?"

"You do ask a lot of questions," said another voice. A sleek little bunny hopped out from a nearby shrub. It was what Dan would have called a Dutch Dwarf rabbit, something he knew only because his sister had once kept a pair of them. Its fur was one shade lighter than chocolate, its ears only a couple of inches long. Two rabbits of its size could easily have fit into Dan's hand.

The llama turned toward the bunny and said, "We were having a very nice conversation until you hopped in."

"Excuse me for breathing." The bunny cocked its little head up toward Dan and said, "Stick out your tongue and say ah."

"What?"

"Never mind." The bunny inspected him, then declared, "You look fairly alive to me. As alive as anybody would, after a first-class fall like that."

Dan poked himself in the arm. "I feel alive."

The bunny and the llama exchanged glances. "He must have hit his head pretty hard," the llama said.

"I guess he could have fallen harder," the bunny agreed. "But only if he had climbed a tree and taken a nose dive off the top branch."

"I hurt too much to be dead," Dan decided.

"I never knew anybody could fall off a horse that hard," the bunny went on.

"Fall off a what?" Dan asked.

"Maybe it's really something else," the llama offered. "A minute ago he was asking where he could find something. I think he called it a *van*."

The bunny elongated its neck as far as it would go, looked down the hillside behind Dan, and said, "Well, it sure looks like a horse to me."

"Could be a spell," the llama said doubtfully.

Dan turned slowly around and looked down the hill. Sure enough, there calmly cropping grass was a horse.

But it was not just any old horse. Dan found himself looking at a white stallion of truly magnificent proportions. One with a coat so shiny it shimmered in the reflected sunlight. The horse was saddleless.

"Your horse doesn't seem all that concerned about you," the bunny observed.

"It was standing over him and watching," the llama replied, "until it heard the young man groan and roll over. Then it walked over there."

Dan raised an understandably shaky hand and pointed downhill. "I was riding that?"

"I suppose you could call it riding," the bunny said doubtfully.

"But I can't ride," Dan protested. "I've never been on a horse in my life. Much less one the size of an elephant. And bareback to boot."

The horse whinnied loud and long, snorted, and cantered off down the hill.

"Uh-oh," the llama observed. "I don't think someone was very pleased to be compared to an elephant."

"I sure wouldn't be," the tiny rabbit agreed.

Dan drew up his knees, set his elbows on top of them, and lowered his head into his hands. "I must be crazy."

The bunny hummed a comment too soft for Dan to catch the words.

"Napoleon, Eleander," called a girl's voice as beautiful as silver chimes. "Where are you?"

A young lady with long golden hair and cornflower blue eyes came into view. "Ah, there you are."

Dan tried to rise to his feet as she approached, but his legs refused to accept the burden. He subsided with a groan.

The girl hastened up the final rise, concern creasing her lovely features. "What is the matter?"

"He fell off his horse," the llama explained. "Or *van*, I'm not sure which."

"You should have seen it," the bunny said. Then he demonstrated, rising up on his hind legs, stiffening suddenly, and keeling over. "Bang, like he was hit by a lightning bolt."

"Oh, you poor man." The girl gathered up her long dress, which was the color of a noonday sky, and knelt beside him. Close up she was more beautiful still. "Are you all right?"

"He asked me if he was dead," the llama reported.

"Where is his horse?"

"Down the hill, see?" The bunny pointed with one of its tiny forepaws. "It got mad when the man here compared it to an elephant."

"I did not," Dan protested.

"Ah, but at least you retain the faculty of speech," the girl said. "That is a good sign for one who has fallen from great heights." She shaded her eyes and looked downhill. "My, but that is a glorious steed. You must be a knight, to ride one such as this."

The bunny snickered into its paws.

"Hush, Napoleon. You know it is not nice to treat strangers thus." She turned to the llama and said, "Eleander, run ask Cook for something to eat. A body needs good food to help it repair."

"Right away, Bliss."

"That's your name?" Dan asked. "Bliss?"

"Yes."

"It suits you perfectly," he declared. And it did.

She dimpled. "Such kind words from a gallant knight."

The bunny placed its tiny forepaws upon its breast and heaved a romantic sigh.

"Are you ailing?" Bliss asked.

"Everywhere, but it's getting better," Dan replied. "Where am I?"

"Ah, a gallant knight from other lands," she said, nodding as though it all made perfect sense. "Have you traveled far?"

Dan looked around at the alien landscape and replied, "Farther than I know how to explain."

"What are you called?"

"Dan," he replied. "Dan Simmons."

"Dansimmons is an uncommon name for these lands where you now stand," Bliss observed.

"Or sit," the bunny corrected. "Whatever."

"Dansimmons falls strange from the tongue," Bliss continued, ignoring the rabbit. "You are indeed from distant lands; I can tell that by the strangeness of your speech."

Dan could only nod. Distant lands.

"Dansimmons is not a name that suits you." She brightened. "I know. We will call you Daniel. It is an ancient name, one taken by a great knight, a man who lived in a time called hopeless by his people. Yet still he rose high in an alien kingdom and did well for his people. It is a story I know from the Book."

"I think I heard that story when I was a kid," Dan said. "Or at least one pretty much like it."

"Here you are, Bliss," the llama said, trotting back into view, a haversack slung around its neck.

"Oh, thank you, Eleander." Bliss unslung the bag, opened it, and handed over a sandwich so thick it filled his hand. "Here, gallant knight. Eat, and may your strength return swiftly."

"Thank you." He took a bite and announced, "Delicious."

The dimples returned. "Cook will be pleased." She pulled a drinking flask from the haversack and set it upon the grass between them. "Then Daniel you shall be. Yes?"

His mouth being very full, Dan replied with a nod. Her beauty and her eager expression left little room for disagreement.

"Oh, splendid." She clapped her hands. "Oh, I do so love a naming."

"It usually takes a lot longer," the llama observed. "You took three whole days for me."

"Yes, but I couldn't detain such a gallant knight for so long," Bliss replied.

Dan swallowed, debated whether he should confess to not being a knight, then decided there was no need to disappoint her. Instead he asked, "Do all animals talk here?"

The llama and the bunny exchanged glances. The bunny said, "What a goofball."

"Napoleon!" The girl was plainly shocked. "Did I teach you to talk like that?"

"Somebody had to," the bunny replied calmly. "So I guess it must have been you."

The girl sniffed and turned back to Dan. "Of course all animals don't talk. The world would be far too noisy, silly."

"So how come you can call him silly and get away with

it?" the bunny complained. "All I said was—"

"Don't," the girl warned.

Dan stretched out his legs and found the soreness was lessening. "Just what I need," he said. "A bunny with an attitude."

"I taught these two the speech of humans because they are my friends," Bliss explained. "And because I wanted them to be able to know their names."

Her gaze turned shyly downward. "I confess that it is also because I often taste the cup of loneliness and like it not."

"That's hard to believe," the newly renamed Daniel said. "A pretty girl like you ought to have to fight them off with a stick."

Her cheeks colored. "Your speech is strange and at times harsh on the ears, Daniel. Yet I like you. I should like to visit with you some more. Will you come here again?"

"If I can," he replied, wishing the two animals weren't listening to the conversation so attentively. "I'd like to, very much."

"An honest answer," Bliss said, her eyes only for him. "Of course, I should expect nothing less from so gallant a knight."

The bunny snorted.

"Where are you headed, Knight Daniel?"

"I'm not sure," Dan replied, wishing he knew where he was.

"Perhaps I can help," Bliss said. "I know of a very wise man who lives not far from here. If you like, we can visit him and see if perhaps he can show you the way."

Dan thought it over and decided, "That sounds like a good idea. Thanks."

"You are indeed welcome." Her expression turned serious. "I find myself wondering if perhaps you are the one sent to help us with our difficulty."

"You have got to be joking," the bunny protested.

"That is enough, Napoleon," Bliss said, her gaze remaining upon Dan. "Could you tell me why you have come?"

"I don't know," Dan said, "if I can put it into words."

She nodded, as though expecting nothing less. "It is indeed hard to place the greatest of truths into the puny speech of people."

She stood and offered him her hand. "Then let us be off."

Dan rose to his feet like a very old man. He tested each joint carefully before putting his full weight on it. When he was as upright as he could get, he found Bliss staring down the slope to where his horse was slowly making its way uphill. For a panic-stricken moment Dan feared he would be expected to ride. Then he realized that she had no mount. That would be his excuse, to walk alongside her.

"Anyone granted the rights of such a worthy steed must truly be set upon a noble quest," Bliss said.

Was it his imagination, or did the horse lift its head a notch at her words? Dan replied honestly, "I couldn't tell you."

"Ah. A secret quest as well. How romantic." The cornflower blue eyes gave him a look of shy wonder. "No doubt you must be called the greatest of knights in your homeland."

Napoleon laughed behind his paws. Dan inched over, but the bunny took a wise hop in the other direction.

Bliss offered the approaching horse a hand. It nuzzled her, then placed its nose in the crook of her neck. Dan had never been jealous of an animal until that moment. She asked, "Is your home far away?"

"You can't imagine how far," Dan replied.

"A place of great learning and wisdom, no doubt," she said wistfully.

The tiny rabbit snickered again. Dan decided to use the distant trees as goalposts and the bunny as a ball, but Napoleon was too fast for him and slipped behind the girl.

"It's not over yet," Dan promised.

"No, indeed not," Bliss agreed, not understanding. "It has only just begun, and therefore we should not tarry longer. Come."

–THREE–

At this same time, yet far from the place where Bliss and Dan descended the hillside, there lived a young girl. She was growing up in what psychologists might call difficult circumstances. Psychologists are very good at being clinically detached, which means looking at a highly emotional situation with no emotion at all. What it meant to the young girl, whose name was Consuela, was very different from what the psychologist who visited her home every other Thursday saw through her detached, hardened, caseworker eyes.

It was the only childhood Consuela had ever known, so she could not compare herself with other children as the caseworker did. She did not compare her alcoholic mother with mothers who were on drugs or families who had no mother at all. She did not know to be thankful that she was not what the psychologists called a victim of a dangerous environment. She did not know to classify her childhood as a borderline case, which required regular biweekly supervision, or that discussions were made once a quarter about putting her in an overcrowded children's home. Consuela was simply living her childhood the best she could.

Which, all in all, was very well indeed.

Consuela and her mother did not have much money, and the old building where they lived was not very nice. It smelled, and the other people who lived around them were scary to a nine-year-old girl. It was too cold in winter, too hot in summer, and the walls were thin enough to let in all kinds of nasty noises. The street outside was cracked and pitted and lined with hopeless faces. The only green along Consuela's street was the grass struggling to grow up through cracks in the sidewalk. But these things seldom bothered Consuela. How could they? She saw them hardly at all.

Consuela did not remember when she first found the door. It was at night, she knew that. It was years earlier, so long ago that the door was one of her first real memories. At first it had been easier to go through the door when it was dark and the world was quieter and she was safe in her bed. For a while, she could only pass the threshold when she was sleepy. Nowadays, though, it did not matter. The door was open all the time. She skipped in and out of it with ease. She could walk down her street and see only what lay beyond the door. Or she could sit straight in the kitchen chair and fasten her eyes on the caseworker and go dancing off beyond the door. Which was what she was doing now.

The caseworker, who had told Consuela to call her Sally, breathed out smoke in a harsh sigh and stubbed her cigarette in the saucer she was using as an ashtray. "Your mother's going to sleep through the meeting again. Does she do this often, sleep all afternoon?"

Consuela nodded vaguely. She was looking at Sally's long red fingernails and yet seeing the park. That was what she called the green fields that stretched out just beyond the door. There were a lot of trees, enough to be called a forest really, but everything was carefully tended like some enormous private park. The trees stood high and broad and ancient, but each was placed with loving care so that light could fall upon the rich green grass growing between them. Flowers were gentle speckles of color that swayed in careful unison to the warm breeze. The flowers were not planted in bunches. They lay in scattered harmony amidst the park's endless green, growing exactly where they should. Just like the trees.

The caseworker asked doubtfully, "Are you sure you're all right here?"

"Fine." Consuela was having trouble not laughing. She was sitting on the grass, watching the antics of Punk. Punk was a plump green dwarf with bulging eyes and a rooster-crown of bright red hair that stood spiked and straight along the crest of his head.

Punk was flapping his stubby little arms and trying to fly. Two tiny sparrows had hold of his shirt and were fluttering so hard their wings were a blur, trying to help Punk lift off the ground. Punk had been trying to fly the very first time Consuela had met him, which was the first time she had stepped through the door, and it had remained one of her favorite games ever since.

"Well," the caseworker woman sighed, "I guess there's nothing more for me to do today. Tell your mother when she wakes up that I was here and that I'll have to report her. Again."

Consuela nodded and slid from the chair. But because her attention was not on her action, she misjudged the movement. Her feet slid out from under her, and her head struck the table with a solid *thunk*.

Consuela melted down to the floor. Her eyelids fluttered and then were still.

"Oh, don't tell me." The caseworker knelt down beside

the very still, very silent little girl. "Come on, Consuela, wake up. This is no time for fun and games."

Consuela did not move.

The caseworker peeled back an eyelid, then let it drop. Consuela was out like a light. "Great, just great."

The caseworker rose and walked on her sore feet to the telephone. Her eyes remained on Consuela as she dialed the number for the ambulance service. She tried to will Consuela to wake up. But Consuela did not budge.

"Just what I need," the caseworker muttered to herself. "Now I've got to run you to the hospital and fill out more forms. And on a day like this. It's too much." She stood and looked down at the very still little girl, and said to herself, "Maybe it's not too late to go back to school. Study for some easy job like steel working. Or atomic engineering. Come on, Consuela, don't put me through this today, okay?"

The look that came over Consuela caused Punk to stop his antics and ask, "What's wrong?"

"I don't know," Consuela replied. "All of a sudden I feel different."

"How different?"

"I'm not sure," Consuela replied. "Just different."

Punk shooed the sparrows away and walked up closer. "You look the same to me."

She looked down at herself. "Everything seems more, I don't know, real or something."

Punk looked her up and down. "Maybe we better go find Cousteau."

–Four–

The dwelling was too small to be called a true castle. It looked more like a manor upon which someone had attached whimsical towers and turrets and ramparts, all too small for men to use. The windows were narrow and high, the doors stout and oaken. It was a charming place, in a seedy and run-down fashion.

"You must promise to be kind," Bliss told him as they drew near the main entrance.

"Why do you say a thing like that?"

"He is old and feeble and tends to wander in his mind," she said, her eyes sad as she stared upward at the empty ramparts. "But he is still our strongest guardian, when his vision is clear."

"Guardian against what?"

She turned and showed him those beautiful dimples. "There is no need to tell a noble knight of such things."

"No, of course not," Dan agreed, climbing the broad stairs behind her. "So what happens when his vision gets cloudy?"

She lifted the heavy brass knocker and let it fall. The boom echoed far down unseen halls. "Yes," she agreed quietly. "It is at such times that we are in need of a knight such as yourself."

Before he could reply, the door was opened by a green dwarf who was almost as broad as he was tall. His eyes opened wide in surprise. "Bliss! What are you doing here?"

"Hello, Punk," she replied. "I have brought us a noble knight."

"A knight," Punk repeated, inspecting Dan from head to toe, then bowing as deeply as his great girth and small stature would allow. "In the name of my master, and Him whom we all serve, I bid you both peace."

"A fair welcome, Punk, one with which your master would be well pleased." Bliss stepped through the portal.

Dan followed her inside, increasingly uneasy with his charade. But he found it terrifically hard to deny something so important to a lady who was so beautiful.

"Where is Cousteau?" Bliss asked.

The dwarf motioned with his oversized head. "He is entertaining the girl."

"Ah. Perhaps we should go in. How is he?"

The dwarf shrugged. "Comes and goes, my lady, comes and goes."

They walked through a massive entrance hall floored in flagstone and decorated with murals that rose high up the lofty walls. Bliss led Dan toward a pair of closed doors. Peals of bell-like laughter resounded through the portals.

Bliss said quietly, "He has a visitor from time to time. A young girl, also from a distant land. She is called Consuela. Perhaps you know of her?"

"No," Dan replied.

"I thought as not. She is young and carefree, yet does him much good. She loves to laugh." Bliss looked at him with sorrowful eyes. "I only wish he gave as much care to our troubles as he does nowadays to her laughter."

They paused while the dwarf rapped sharply on the doors, then pushed them both open with a flourish. "More visitors, master," he proclaimed.

"Ah, Bliss!" A stooped old man with a long gray beard rose from his low chair. As he did, six dancing balls of light disappeared from the air before him. "How wonderful it is to see you. You are keeping well, my dear?"

"For myself, I have only thanks to give," she replied, bussing his cheek. "But for the world . . ."

"Ah, yes, the world." He sighed. "And an old man frees himself from the worries he can no longer manage with the laughter of this delightful child." The old man turned and smiled benevolently upon the dark-haired little girl. "You remember Bliss, my dear."

"Of course," Consuela replied. "Can we play with the balls some more?"

"Perhaps a bit later." He turned back to eye Dan and ask, "And who is this fine young man?"

"A knight," Bliss replied proudly. "A noble knight from distant lands." She turned and said with gravity, "Knight Daniel, may I introduce Cousteau, Master Weaver and watchman over the Valley of Shadows."

Dan found himself caught in the solemnity of the moment and gave a deep bow.

"Well, well, well." The old man shuffled forward and held out a delicately veined hand. "Help arrives at last. How utterly marvelous. Are you a prince of the realm?"

"I'm afraid not," Dan replied, and confessed, "I'm not even really a knight."

"Modesty from one such as him," Bliss said with pride and affection. "You should see his valiant steed."

"It's not really my horse either," Dan said, wishing he did not have to disappoint them.

"Of course not," Cousteau said approvingly. "No one can

claim possession of another living being, can he?" He peered at Dan with eyes that appeared untouched by his vast years. "You are sure that you are not a prophet or seer or prince from the realm?"

"I don't even know what you are talking about," Dan replied. "All I know is that I was driving along in a snowstorm and I was sideswiped by a truck."

Bliss responded with delightful laughter. "His speech is so quaint at times, is it not?"

"Indeed," the old man agreed. "Much as that of our young maiden." He turned and said, "Perhaps I should introduce my young visitor. Knight Daniel, this is Consuela."

Consuela was staring at him with an unaccustomed frown. "I didn't make you up," she declared.

Both her words and her accent caught him by surprise. "You sound American," he said.

"I am," she replied impatiently. "What are *you* doing in *my* dream?"

"How did you get here?" he asked, hoping for a clue.

"What do you mean, *get* here. I *made* here." She was becoming crosser by the moment. "And I don't think I want you here anymore."

The old man chuckled indulgently. "Think nothing of her words, my son. From time to time she declares me a figment of her imagination as well."

"She is young," Bliss agreed, "and still has much to learn."

"Oh," Consuela spouted in exasperation, "I hate it when you talk about me like that."

The old man said to Dan, "You are here to help us in our hour of desperate need?"

"He is on a noble quest," Bliss replied for him.

"Ah." The old man nodded sagely. "Such things do I recall from my own youth."

"I brought him," Bliss went on, "because in return for his help I thought that we should perhaps offer our own."

"Can we play with the balls some more *now*?" Consuela demanded.

The old man raised his hand for silence. "Forgive my young friend," he said to Dan. "She is a delight to an old man's days."

Dan was still looking at Consuela. "I thought this was *my* dream."

The old man and Bliss exchanged glances.

"Perhaps it is the speech of their homeland," she said doubtfully.

"Dreams within dreams within dreams," the old man sighed. "What I would give for days gone by."

Consuela was still staring at Dan. "I don't think I like you," she declared.

The old man gave her a horrified look. "My child! You must apologize."

"Likewise," Dan replied. "Only double."

Consuela clenched her eyelids tightly shut, poked out her cheeks, froze for a moment, then opened her eyes. Crossly she slapped her hand on her leg. "Why won't you go *away*?"

"Very good question," Dan replied. "Can you tell me where I am?"

"You are," Cousteau replied with sudden formality, "standing upon the border of the Kingdom of Shadows."

Bliss helped the old man climb the narrow stone stairs, which wound around and around and around. They climbed to a height far above anything Dan imagined the manor might contain.

"Cousteau is our greatest weaver," Bliss was saying

from up ahead. Her voice echoed up and down the stone-lined stairwell.

Dan imagined hand-loomed baskets and blankets. "How nice."

"These days, not many are interested in learning the discipline of light weaving," the old man said, making heavy going of the tower. "It is an art that is slowly vanishing."

"Light weaving?" Dan asked.

"It is a most difficult task," Bliss told him, her strides slowing to match those of Cousteau. "Most especially because one must seek beyond the mind and the senses for answers, a challenge which proves too much for most. Including myself."

"Nonsense," the old man snorted. "You were simply granted gifts in other directions."

"Teaching animals the speech of humans is scarcely something that might save us in this hour of need."

"Do not belittle your gifts, my daughter," Cousteau chided. "You can never tell what great and glorious part might await you just around the next bend."

"Light weaving," Dan muttered to himself. Now he had definitely heard everything.

"He has tried to teach me," Bliss said over her shoulder. "But I failed to learn."

"Not so, not so," Cousteau retorted loudly. "She weaves with her heart, with each breath, with each word she teaches her precious charges. She was simply not given the task of weaving for man's eyes to see. And because her work remains unseen to all but those willing to open their hearts to the songs of heaven, she calls herself ungifted." The old man snorted. "For such nonsense I have no patience."

Dan noticed how the little girl called Consuela was hanging back and sulking, kicking her toes angrily against each step as she climbed.

He waited for her to catch up. "Something the matter?"

"I don't want to go up there. I want to stay down and play with the balls. Where's Punk?"

"Punk is guarding the door," Cousteau replied patiently. "It is high time you saw more than my parlor tricks."

"I don't want to," she said, but continued along just the same.

Dan lowered his voice and asked quietly, "Where are you from?"

"No place you'd know," she retorted. "And why haven't you gone like I told you to?"

"Good question," Dan replied. "But I'd still like to know where you're from."

"I've told you and told you and told you to leave, and still you're here," she said crossly. "I don't like this at all."

"Remember your manners," Cousteau called from beyond the stairs' rising curve.

Consuela looked up at Dan and said, "Who are you anyway?"

"Dan Simmons," he replied. "Formerly of Baltimore."

Her eyes opened wide. "That's where I'm from. Why would I dream you here?"

"This is too much," Dan replied.

"Ah, finally," the old man cried. "I had forgotten just how far it was."

"Which also says how long it has been," Bliss said worriedly. "If you do not keep guard, who does?"

"My dear," Cousteau puffed. "I find that as I grow older and these eyes become dimmer, the heart's vision becomes much sharper. I no longer need to stand at these heights in order to see the trouble ahead."

Bliss was not convinced. "Perhaps also you choose to ignore troubles with parlor tricks and a child's laughter."

"I am *not* a child," Consuela said, stomping up the final

stairs to the landing. "Oooh, this is nice."

Dan stopped and looked out over a broad green valley. It looked pleasant enough at first glance, but there was a certain lack of harmony in the scene. The heat rose in shimmering waves, making it difficult to focus upon anything very clearly. From what he could make out, the distant forest and fields were like those he was accustomed to. Trees grew in clustered profusion, pressing up against the borders of hard-won fields, ever ready to reclaim the land taken by man. Birds swooped from tree to tree, their distant songs chiming in the crisp air.

"This doesn't look like a bad place at all," Consuela declared, peering out over the parapet.

The old man peered fondly down upon her dark hair. "The best of illusions," he replied, "are those which fool the eye with promises of a peace that is not there."

"No doubt our noble knight can see through to the truth beyond," Bliss said proudly. "Although I confess that it is difficult even for me to see where truth ends and night begins."

"No doubt," Cousteau agreed, peering at Dan with eyes filled with uncommon wisdom. He reached out a feeble hand. "Grant me the strength of your young shoulder, would you?"

"Sure." Dan moved forward and allowed the old man to lean upon him.

Suddenly there was a sense of a veil lifting. Dan realized that the shimmering confusion was not caused by heat at all, but rather by some unwelcome force. It was not a realization of the senses. He felt it in his bones, in the chill that suddenly gripped his very being. Dan looked out over the landscape and saw what had been hidden before—high banks of looming clouds encircling the land, forces gathering for an onslaught, a power seeking to conquer and control.

"Ah," Cousteau murmured. "Our young knight shows the ability to see beneath the Dark King's mask."

Dan shivered.

Immediately Cousteau released his shoulder and said, "Indeed it as you say, Bliss. We are most fortunate to have one such as he among us." He patted Dan's back. "Come, let us descend to the comforts of hearth and home."

When they had returned to the central hall, Bliss said, "The knight must no doubt be setting off upon his quest."

"Good," Consuela said crossly. "I still don't understand why he's got to be here at all."

"Be still, my child," Cousteau said gently and rested a knowing gaze upon Bliss. "Perhaps," he suggested, "our noble guest might be willing to have a friend and guide take him as far as Borderland."

Bliss brightened immediately. She turned to Dan and said, "Would you?"

"Only if it's you," Dan replied.

"Puull-leasse," Consuela said and stomped back into the parlor.

"We have friends who dwell there," Cousteau said.

"Of course," Bliss said excitedly. "They can help you. Why did I not think of that myself?"

"Because your mind was on other matters," Cousteau replied, tugging at his beard in order to hide his smile.

"I need all the help I can get," Dan said. "Especially yours."

"In that case," Cousteau said, "before you go I wish to show you something else, so that you might depart from here with a vision of Light foremost in your memory, rather than one of illusion and shadow." He turned and said, "Be so kind as to follow me."

"Do you think now is the proper time?" Bliss asked doubtfully.

The old man raised his chin to a lofty level. "Of things such as these, I have no room for doubt."

"But he has so much already to concern himself over," Bliss said.

"When, if not now?" Cousteau shuffled forward, not awaiting a reply. "He must continue with his quest. And who knows, perhaps a glimpse into the unseen will help him face what comes."

They took a different stairway this time, one which seemed to *carry* him upward. Dan felt himself lifted more by a lightness of the air than by his own legs.

The great doors at the top of the stairs were open. As he approached, the old man said, "This portal is always welcoming. The question is, who is willing to enter?"

The room was bare except for a great central dais. Upon this raised stone platform lay what appeared to be both a book and a beacon.

Dan approached hesitantly, remaining behind the old man.

Cousteau, on the other hand, appeared to grow younger with each step, younger and taller and straighter and stronger. "This is the Book of Light," he proclaimed, "open to all who care to see, open to all who see in order to understand."

He turned back the great cover, and Dan felt himself illuminated from within. Yet he could not read the page. The light streaming forth was too strong.

"I can't see," he complained.

"It is because you seek to see with your eyes," Cousteau replied.

"I don't know what you are talking about," Dan said, but at the same time seemed to hear a faint voice calling to him from within his own heart. A voice that yearned. A voice that hungered. A voice that invited him to seek and delve deeper.

"Here and here alone you must allow yourself to be guided by the One whose Presence is found upon the page."

Dan started to argue, then caught himself. He felt as though a second set of eyes was gradually opening within himself, somewhere deep inside. But still he could not see. For it felt as though he had a veil cast between his heart and the Book, and the veil was made from all that was untrue within himself. All the lies he told to himself and to others. All the misdeeds of his life. All the paths he had taken that were tainted by selfish desires.

Dan stood and looked down at the page and felt himself watching both inward and outward at the same time. He felt at peace, and yet enormously troubled, for the mirror shone with boundless love and yet illuminated much within himself that he did not wish to see.

"Enough," the old man said and closed the book. "For now, that is enough."

Dan was both relieved and sorrowful as he followed Cousteau back down the stairs.

Bliss was waiting for them at the landing, concern etched deeply upon her features. "Are you all right?"

"I'm not sure," Dan replied weakly.

"Honest even when shaken by the power of Truth," Cousteau said approvingly. "I am sure that your feet will remain steadfast upon the Way, noble knight, even when all around you is cloaked in darkest night."

–FIVE–

Dr. Prain walked the long hospital corridor, feeling fairly content with his existence.

His hated emergency room tour was behind him for good. He had the chief administrator's solemn word to that effect. He was back on his cherished duty as staff doctor to a ward.

The hospital was less than six months old and still had the fresh-paint newness and shine. Dr. Prain's immaculate ward was the one small section of the world that ran according to his all-important principles. The ward was orderly. Clean. Functional. Precise. And on his ward all questions had logical answers.

For Dr. Prain, happiness was another word for being in control.

There was only one dark cloud on Dr. Prain's horizon that morning. It was the patient in Room 239. The one identified as Dan Simmons.

Dr. Prain took this young man's stubborn refusal to respond to treatment as a personal insult. Over the past two days the doctor had run every test he could think of, then gone back and run some of them a second time.

The results all came back normal.

Dr. Prain was completely and utterly baffled, a state he hated worse than the flu. There was a perfectly good reason for the young man's continued slumber. That Dr. Prain could not discover it was a slap in the face.

Just walking past the door of Room 239 was enough to raise his blood pressure ten points.

His buzzer sounded. He walked to the nearest wall phone and punched in the code shown on the buzzer's display. "Prain."

"Hey, great, what's up?"

"Not much." He recognized the voice of Dr. Sinclair down in ER. "What can I do for you?"

"I'm sending you up another of them."

"Another of them what?"

"Sleepers. Little girl by the name of Consuela, uh, yeah, here it is. Consuela Ortez. Fell and hit her head about four hours ago." There was the sound of pages being flipped. "We've run the usual tests; everything came back normal. We've held her down here so long thinking probably she'd wake up on her own and we could send her home. But the caseworker who brought her in is going off duty. Family situation doesn't sound like something that'll guarantee care and support—father gone, mother incapacitated. Looks like we'll have to keep her here overnight."

Just what he needed, another question mark on his ward. "Sorry, I'm all full up."

"That's funny, I've got you down as having a bed free in 237."

Dr. Prain stifled an oath. Old Mrs. Johnston had finally expired that very morning. "Look, can't you give this one to somebody else?"

"What's the matter?" The ER doctor was growing impatient. "How much trouble is a nine-year-old girl who won't wake up going to give you?"

"It's not that." Dr. Prain knew there was nothing he could do about it. He sighed in defeat. "Okay. Send her on up."

"Already on the way. Orderly should be there any minute." A siren sounded in the background. "Gotta run. See ya."

Dr. Prain hung up the phone. He had a fleeting image of these patients becoming his own personal legacy. Jack Prain, the doctor who couldn't get his patients to wake up. What a nightmare. He walked on down the ward, feeling the walls of rigid control shuddering slightly.

– Six –

"What's this place where we're headed?" Dan asked Bliss.

"Borderland is not a place," Bliss replied. "It is a town."

Dan had avoided revealing his lack of horsemanship in a most gallant fashion, insisting that Bliss ride instead. Bliss had replied with a curtsey and the grave thanks of one who had expected nothing less from her noble knight.

They traveled a forest path full of green-tinted sunshine, birdsong, and the fragrance of flowers. Dan walked alongside the horse, so that from time to time his shoulder grazed against the lady's leg.

Somehow the horse seemed to help her ride, just as it had aided her in mounting. Dan could not explain it, but still he felt that it was so. There was neither saddle nor bridle upon the horse because none was needed. The horse simply made it so.

"Borderland is a town built at a crossroads," Bliss went on. "It is said that the people who live there are neither hot nor cold, neither this nor that, and thus are the worst of all."

"Yet you have friends there?"

"Not I. Cousteau. Cousteau has friends everywhere. At least, everywhere I have traveled. His name will sometimes reach the hearts of people who otherwise are touched only by gold."

Dan recalled his visit to the chamber and said, "I think I know what you mean."

"Of course you do," she said, smiling down at him. "That is part of what makes you a knight."

"I'm not a knight," Dan confessed, shattered by his need for her to know the truth.

"You are a knight and you are noble," she calmly replied. "I have seen it in my heart of hearts and thus know it to be true."

"I wish it were," Dan said, then added softly, "for you."

"Does the thought not call to you?" She watched him with a gaze left untouched by his denial. "Do you not wish your life were filled with a higher purpose? A calling worthy of a life lived to the fullest?"

"Yes," he confessed. "Often."

"Then accept that it is so," she said, and cut off further talk by raising her hand and pointing ahead. "Look. We have arrived."

The village was a ramshackle affair. Hovels and shanties stood amidst larger businesses whose windows displayed crude wares. There were feed stores and blacksmiths and dry goods and many shops that appeared to sell only weapons—swords and shields and spears and bows and knives. Music tinkled from the open doors of numerous bars. Raised walkways made of rough-cut planks kept the pedestrians out of the churned and dusty streets.

Corrals for horses and other animals spanned most free spaces. Dan and Bliss stopped at a stable run by a bowlegged little man whose face bore a distinct resemblance to his charges. Bliss slipped from the horse's back, spoke with the man, then returned to Dan and said, "Your steed will be safe here."

"That's more than I can say for myself," Dan said, casting an eye at the passersby. Almost every man was armed with at least a long-bladed knife, and walked with the casual swagger of those who accepted living and dying by force.

"Yes," Bliss agreed. "Safety is a luxury in these lands. Come."

She moved up close to Dan's side. Having her draw so near made him feel ten feet tall, despite the challenging looks cast his way.

The streets were crowded, as were the boardwalks. Most people looked as rough as the town. Dan bent his head down close to Bliss and asked, "Why is everyone staring at me? You, I can understand. But why me?"

"Because you wear no sign upon you," she replied.

"No what?"

"Sign," she repeated. "You bear no weapons, yet you carry yourself erect as a knight should. You bear neither badge of allegiance nor colors of honor. You have no robes of priestly safety, yet you carry nothing with which to defend yourself."

"I think I understand," he said.

"And," Bliss added, "a maiden draws near and looks to you for her defense."

"A fair maiden," he amended. "Very fair."

She dimpled and said, "Your words are most kind, Daniel. Yet we must put such thoughts aside for now. Here there is great danger, and thus we must show care and constant vigilance."

"And just what am I supposed to do if someone attacks us?" Dan held up his empty hands. "Shout?"

"That shall now be attended to," she replied.

She led him down a muddy side street and into a shop that was little more than a log hut. It leaned wearily against its neighbor. It showed the street a single window so begrimed it was impossible to tell what was within.

Bliss rapped sharply and pushed aside a door hung on stout leather hinges. "Leon?" she called. "Are you at home?"

"Who's there?" A grizzled man slapped aside a rear hanging and stepped into view. "Oh," he grunted. "It's you."

Bliss stepped back. "Is that any way to greet an old friend?"

"Is it any way for an old friend to act," he retorted crossly, "not to show her face for months on end?"

She was instantly contrite. "I wanted to come, Leon. Truly I did. But Cousteau has not been up to such a journey for quite some time. And you know I could not attempt it alone."

He gave a sharp nod of acceptance. "And how is the weaver?"

"Old," Bliss replied. "And growing more so with each passing day."

"Then all is lost," the man declared grimly.

"Not so," Bliss replied, motioning Dan forward. "I bring with me a friend. May I present the Knight Daniel? This is Leon, Master Craftsman."

Dan looked at Leon. He was short, and his bald pate was wreathed by wiry silver-gray hair. The rest of the man was as hairy as an aging bear. A thick crop of gray grew from his arms and face and sprouted from the top of his leather apron. He was not a big man, but looked solid as a tree trunk and hard as iron.

Leon inspected Dan with a skeptical eye. "A knight, you say? Where are his weapons? His armor?"

"His need for weaponry is what has brought us here," Bliss replied.

Dan spotted a set of spears propped in the far corner. Beside them stood several dusty sabers. He said, "Can we hang on just a second?"

"As for armor," Bliss continued, "he has need of none."

"Excuse me?" Dan said.

Leon remained unimpressed. He cast a doubtful eye upon Dan's lanky frame and said, "He has no need for muscles either, I suppose. Nor for the seasoning of age."

"He has strength sufficient for ten," Bliss replied smugly, "and knows the wisdom which is ever ageless."

"Time out," Dan said.

"We'll see," Leon said and reached behind him. He came up with a pair of swords, one of which he tossed to Dan. "Let's see what you can do, lad."

"That is the last time you shall ever use the word 'lad' when referring to our new friend," Bliss predicted.

Dan looked down at his sword. To his utter surprise, he had caught it by its hilt. He said, "This won't take long."

"Do not hurt the man overmuch," Bliss warned, misunderstanding Dan. "He is a friend."

Leon snorted and hefted his blade. "He is like no knight I have ever known. And all I have seen thus far is his willingness to allow a woman to speak for him."

Dan started to tell him to remember what Bliss had said about injury, but stopped when he raised his own sword. For some reason it appeared to fit. More than that. Dan hefted the blade and knew it as well as he knew the fingers of his own hand.

He had never held a blade before in his entire life.

"En garde!" the grizzled craftsman cried, and attacked.

Dan parried the blow without batting an eye. It would

be hard to say who was more surprised, Dan or the crafts-man.

Leon homed in closer with a flurry of blows.

Dan responded with nothing more than blade and hand and wrist.

Leon backed off a pace, sweating and blowing hard. "Do not insult me so," he cried. "If it must be done, let it be with honor."

"Okay," Dan agreed. "Let's see how far this goes."

He moved with the assuredness of one born to the blade. He set his body into position, planted his front foot, stepped forth, balanced, and attacked.

Leon's sword went flying across the room.

"Hold," the older man puffed.

"And you thought to challenge my words," Bliss scolded. "You thought to call the knight a lad."

"Never have I seen such power in one so young of years," the craftsman proclaimed, a new light in his eyes. "Perhaps it is as you say."

"There is indeed hope anew," Bliss agreed.

Leon asked him, "How are you with the bow and throw-ing knives?"

"I don't know," Dan replied.

"At times he relies overmuch on modesty," Bliss ex-plained. "It is perhaps his greatest failing."

"Follow me," Leon said, and led them under the back flap.

Behind the shop was an elaborate smithy's forge, and beyond that lay a small field. The green expanse was planted with various posts and hanging sacks for testing equipment.

"He is too small for handling a broadsword," Leon de-clared, "no matter what you might say."

"You assuredly would know best, Master Craftsman,"

Bliss replied, showing Dan her dimples.

Leon busied himself rummaging through a clutter of weaponry and drawing forth numerous articles, which he laid upon a trestle table. He dived into a shadowy corner, then emerged holding a bow longer than he was high. "But perhaps his wiry frame might contain the force for this."

"Do not make fun of the knight," Bliss warned. "You have already seen his prowess with the blade."

"What think you, knight?" Leon demanded, ignoring Bliss. "Could you best such a bow?"

"Only one way to find out," Dan replied, willing to try anything now.

"The bow was meant for one twice your size," Bliss said concernedly. "The craftsman jests where jests are not welcome."

"Let him try," Leon said.

Dan took the bow and sensed a joining. A powerful energy hummed through the unstrung bow, melding it to his fist. Instantly he knew what was to be done.

"Give me a string," Dan said.

When the craftsman handed one over, Dan twined the bow around his leg, bracing it against his foot. He did not pull it down with his arm; rather he leaned with it, using the strength of his entire body to bend the bow and string it.

Once this was done, he plucked the string once, feeling the hum race up his arm, sounding throughout his entire frame. "Arrows?"

Soundlessly the craftsman handed him a full quiver.

Again Dan knew exactly what to do. He walked around the table, selected three arrows, planted them firmly in the earth at his feet. He pulled out a fourth, set the quiver aside, raised the bow, and set the arrow into place.

He drew and aimed and shot with the fluidity of water racing downstream.

Before the string had ceased its hum, the second arrow was set into place and shot after the first. The third was let loose before the second struck the target. The fourth followed as one word does another from a singer's lips.

All four landed within a handsbreadth of one another, forming a diamond pattern upon the field's farthest post.

Leon raced over, laughed aloud, and shouted back to them, "By the stars, he has split the post with each!"

He returned empty-handed. "For all who come and question the right of one such as this to bear my arms, I shall point to those arrows and tell this tale," he proclaimed. "They shall remain where they are for as long as I myself am alive."

Dan unstrung the bow. "I like the feel of this one."

"Aye, knight, and the bow likes the feel of you." He pointed to the table and demanded, "The short knives or long?"

"Your guess is as good as mine," Dan replied, walking over.

The longer knives were slender and the length of his forearm, the entire blade a gradually tapering point. Without picking them up, Dan knew. He did not understand how or why, yet he *knew*. These were point blades and were balanced to perfection. The shorter blades had sharpened edges running high up each side, and the handles were protected by great metal sheaths.

"The next post but one," Leon said, his eyes still agleam. "Over your left shoulder. Go!"

Like a coiled spring suddenly released, Dan grasped the two long blades, one in each hand. He turned and began a windmill spin at the same moment, letting fly with the force of his entire body behind the throws. Before the second blade had struck he had spun back to the table for the pair of shorter knives. He turned with another controlled swinging cast and fired them off.

The blades struck with solid *thunks*, one beneath the other, a straight line down the heart of the post.

Leon released an explosive breath and repeated, "By the stars above."

Only Bliss remained unaffected by the show of force. She looked deep at Dan and said with unruffled calm, "To be strong enough to know weakness is the greatest strength there is."

Although her words were meant as a compliment, they struck him with the force of an ax upon a tree. Dan could only stand and stare at her, and yearn.

Leon shattered the moment by clapping a hoary hand upon Dan's shoulder. "Come, Knight Daniel. There is a sword within that has been awaiting your hand."

– SEVEN –

"A knight is a knight," Bliss said, her tone resigned. "He is what he is, and is called by times such as these. And yet I wish it were otherwise."

Leaving the craftsman, Dan and Bliss had stopped to see a leatherworker who had fitted him out from head to toe. Now and then, when the crowds lightened momentarily, Dan cast an astonished glance down his front.

They had equipped him well.

He wore boots that climbed halfway up his calves, yet were so supple he could have balled them up like socks. Suede pants the color of autumn leaves. Padded leather vest with silver studs for fastening the leather cross-straps. Matching silver and leather guards for his wrists.

And that was only the start.

In his left hand he carried the unstrung longbow, with two quivers strapped along its length. The quivers were of stout leather, dressed in ingrained silver, as was the bow itself. A sword nestled within its gleaming scabbard slapped comfortably against his left leg in time to each step. The two long-bladed throwing knives were crossed behind his back, their hilts rising far enough for him to reach and grab and throw in one smooth motion. One of the shorter knives rested in a sheath strapped to his left wrist, the other to his right ankle.

Dan felt like a medieval version of a fully loaded F–14.

Now that Dan was armed, the attitude shown him by others was very, very different. No longer did he and Bliss have to struggle along the overcrowded lane. A space was made for them. People made note of his stance and his arms, and most chose to give way immediately, their eyes downcast, their attitude servile.

Except for a few.

Most of the other pedestrians bearing warrior's arms, rather than a single sword or dagger for self-defense, did so with grace. Those Dan passed often met his eye with a humorous gaze, silently mocking one so young who bore such weaponry.

Yet there were others who eyed him as prey, and went out of their way to jostle him. Dan found it hard to hold faith in his unexplained talents when confronted with men twice his size, who bore their scars from previous battles like badges of honor. Bliss greeted these overt challenges with a sad silence, which brought him low as well. So Dan swallowed his anger and averted his eyes.

When he refused these challenges, the warriors would often laugh aloud, giving a derisive call before sauntering off. Dan swiftly learned to spot those types before they spotted him, by the look in their eyes and by their swaggering gait. He tried to hold a distance as they passed, but it was not always possible.

It was this reaction of his which had caused Bliss to speak. "I know you will be required to accept such a challenge in order to establish your name," she went on. "And yet how I wish it could be otherwise."

"So do I," Dan agreed, chilled by the fear that this talent which had been so easily gained might just as swiftly be lost.

Bliss looked at him with undisguised approval. "It is a mark of wisdom to choose your first challenger with care," she said. "Afterwards, people will recall your desire to avoid these disputes. Those who challenged you will be made lesser, and you the greater."

"I wish I were half the man you think I am," Dan replied.

"You are twice that and more," Bliss said, "and continue to surprise me with all that you know."

The town's central square was hot and dusty and little different from the rest of Borderland. The buildings surrounding the plaza were adorned with a first floor of stone, giving it a more solid, permanent air.

"We shall take quarters here, such as they are," Bliss said, pointing toward the largest of the structures. "We must have you fit and rested for your quest, and I should not like to make my return journey in the dark."

The square was lined in the same dusty stone as the buildings. At its center rose a large well, sheltered by two ancient trees. Their dusty leaves offered the only green Dan had seen since entering the town.

The people lounging about the square were decidedly less scruffy than those elsewhere, but no less dangerous. As Dan led Bliss down the boardwalk, a trio of men rose from their bench to block his way.

"A pup has dared to steal his master's arms," the tallest one sneered.

"Stand aside and let us pass," Bliss ordered sharply.

"And harbors a lass who knows not when to hold her tongue," the tall man continued. He was dressed in dark trousers and a whitish shirt that appeared to change colors as he moved. A blackened badge in the shape of a serpent was tied to his shoulder by a leather band twined with silver. His hair was as long and dark as the badge. "Such insolence must be taught manners."

"I have no wish to fight you," Dan said. He struggled to force the words past a heart beating like a hummingbird's wings.

"Yet fight me you shall," the tall man sneered, "or else I shall strip you of your finery without a struggle, thus denying you a final taste of honor." He cast a languid eye toward Bliss. "In either case, I shall take the lass for myself. Perhaps she would find the treatment of a real man to be worth remembering."

The threat had a steadying effect. "The lady is her own mistress and goes with whom she pleases," Dan replied.

The anger in Dan's voice brought a gleam to the tall man's eyes. His sneer broadened. "She is a likely-looking wench and should provide a decent night's entertainment," he said.

"That's where you're wrong," Dan replied, finding strength and a quiet focusing in his anger.

"Think you so?" The tall man sighed in mock despair. "A pity to draw my sword for a trifling such as this, but if the lout is permitted to strut as though he truly were a knight, what would the world come to?"

"Chaos," one of his comrades offered.

"Anarchy," the other agreed, shaking his head in mock solemnity.

"Then judgment is cast," the tall one said, and stepped from the boardwalk into the square. He motioned grandly to Dan. "Come, young lout, and receive your comeuppance. That is, if your legs can still carry you."

Dan offered Bliss's hand a firm squeeze before releasing it. Then he handed her his bow and quivers, dropped his leather satchel, and stepped into the full sunlight. "I have no wish to fight you," he repeated.

"Come, come, you begin to bore me," the tall man said, strutting for the benefit of the swiftly gathering crowd. "Would anyone care to take up this lout's charge and make the game a bit more interesting? No, I thought as not. Pity."

The tall man turned back to Dan and showed mock surprise. "What? Still unarmed? Or perhaps you have not yet learned how to draw your weapon." He pointed an indifferent hand. "Grasp that thing there by your side and pull."

"I was just waiting for you to finish your little dance," Dan replied. He was rewarded with a chuckle from the throng.

"The pup has spirit," one of the man's comrades called.

"Perhaps," the tall man said, his face hardening. "But he shall pay dearly for his insolence." His blade rang from its scabbard. "En garde!"

Dan unsheathed his own blade in a slow movement, feeling the hum of metal against metal up through his hand and arm and shoulder to his surging heart. The prowess was there as soon as his hand touched the sword's hilt.

But instead of raising the blade in defense, he lowered the point until it almost touched the stone at his feet.

"Yes," the tall man leered, "it is indeed a heavy burden for one wrapped in fear. Pity your first lesson in courage shall be your last."

Dan remained motionless.

The tall man waved his blade within a foot of Dan's face. "Do you not wish even to try, pup? No? Very well. Then tell your wench farewell!"

Upon his last word, the man leaped.

Dan was no longer there.

The man skidded and spun to find Dan standing in the same posture, his sword at ease, two feet farther to the right. Dan slowly slid his one foot around so that again he faced his opponent.

The crowd murmured its surprise.

The tall man wasted no further words. His lips parted in a fierce grimace as he leapt and plunged again.

And once more met only air.

He cried in fury, raised his sword, and attacked.

Dan finally raised his own blade, met the onslaught, and held his ground.

Steel sang upon steel. The tall man's hair spun out in a great black wreath about his head as he parried and thrust and sought to drive his blade home.

Dan did not attack. He did not flinch. He simply allowed the man to wear himself down. And did not give an inch.

The square was soon filled with the tall man's hoarse breathing. Each blow became matched by an explosive grunt. The man's beautiful shirt was drenching wet and matted tightly to his body.

The surrounding throng had long since become utterly still.

Exhaustion finally forced the challenger to stop. The hand that held his blade trembled violently as it sank toward the earth. He stood with shoulders heaving, his hair disheveled and falling lank around his bowed head.

Dan stepped back and sheathed his sword. The crowd parted in silence to allow him passage.

As he climbed back onto the boardwalk, his opponent cried in a hoarse and broken voice, "You can not leave me like this."

Dan took his bow from a wide-eyed Bliss. "Why not?"

"You have left me robbed of my honor," the man cried.

"You did it to yourself," Dan replied, offering his arm to Bliss. "I told you from the beginning that I didn't want to fight."

–Eight–

"You say the Simmons boy still hasn't woken up?"

"Not even come close to the surface," Dr. Prain replied, lengthening his stride to keep up with the neurosurgeon. "The only time he moves is when the nurses roll him over."

Desperation had forced Dr. Prain to abandon his pride and approach Bob Meadows, the hospital's chief brain specialist. Dr. Meadows was a man of advancing years, kept young by an ever-hungry zest for his profession. There was nothing Dr. Meadows loved more than something new. Which placed him at the exact opposite end of the spectrum from Dr. Prain.

"How long did you say it's been?"

"Over four days." Dr. Prain checked his watch. "To be precise, coming up on four days and six hours."

"That's too long. Far too long." Bob Meadows sounded almost gleeful. "Notify his next of kin?"

"There doesn't appear to be any. Well, there is a sister, but she's on a round-the-world trip with no fixed itinerary. Parents both deceased. No other relatives that the university knows of."

"College kid, is he?" Bob Meadows broke off to stop by

the nurses' station. "Well, hello, Elvira. How's life been treating you?"

"Can't complain, Dr. Meadows, can't complain." The nurse's voice was a full octave lower than the doctor's, and her smile exposed a mouth that appeared to have twice as many teeth. "How's it been with you?"

"Not bad. If I could only find a way to grow me a second set of hands, I might be able to stay on top of things." He patted the countertop. "You take care now."

"Sure will, Dr. Meadows. Nice seeing you again."

"Elvira's a real prize," Dr. Meadows proclaimed, as he and Dr. Prain continued on down the hallway. "You're lucky to be working with someone so capable and concerned."

Dr. Prain replied with a noncommittal grunt. He had not yet made up his mind about Elvira.

"Yes, four days is far too long. You should have called me in sooner."

Dr. Prain's retort was cut off by Dr. Meadows pushing briskly through the door to Room 239. He marched up to the bedside, surveyed the supine form, and proclaimed, "My first impression is that this young fellow is having himself a good snooze."

The patient did his best to agree by emitting a gentle snore.

"For four and a half days?" Dr. Prain countered.

"Hmmm. Yes." Dr. Meadows began his examination. "Skin color excellent. Ditto pupils." He moved farther down. "Reflexes normal. Palpitations indicate nothing out of the ordinary." He went back up and gently rotated the head. "No signs of any abnormality. Just as you indicated." Dr. Meadows took a step back and crossed his arms. "Well, this is a real head-scratcher."

"I've run everything from CT-scan to a blood test for

sleeping sickness," Dr. Prain said, "and come up with a great big egg."

"You say he was involved in an accident and struck his head?"

"That's right. The night of that awful snowstorm. His van was hit by a truck. From the sounds of things, he's lucky to be alive."

"Did you notice whether any glass was imbedded in his scalp?"

Dr. Prain shook his head decisively. "I checked thoroughly. At no point was the skin even lacerated. There was a small bump on his forehead, but even that has almost disappeared. You can still see a faint shadow."

"Yes." Dr. Meadows gently probed the region. "No sign of a hairline fracture?"

"None that I could see. Spine looks perfect as well. I've got the X-ray plates set up across the hall for your inspection. CT-scan and sonogram also."

"Fine." Dr. Meadows straightened as much as his bowed frame would allow. He frowned over the young man's slumbering form, glanced at the monitors attached to the patient and back to the slumbering form. "I don't mind telling you. This one has me flummoxed."

"You can't imagine how relieved I am to hear that."

"There's always the chance that a small amount of blood has leaked into his cranial sack and is exerting pressure upon the brain." Dr. Meadows thrust out his lower lip in concentration. "But my gut reaction is that this is not what we have here. And I hate like the dickens to go drilling a hole in what appears to be a perfectly healthy skull."

"Except for the fact—"

"I know, I know." Dr. Meadows thought it over. "Tell you what. Let's give him another twenty-four hours. If he hasn't moved by then, we'll take another look at that possibility."

"Fine," Dr. Prain agreed. At that point he was ready to give his assent to just about anything. Having someone else admit defeat was greatly reassuring.

"And you say there's another one next door?"

"Similar, but not as serious. Apparently she just hit her head on the kitchen table. She keeps giving signs of rising to consciousness but hasn't quite made it yet."

"Interesting," Dr. Meadows murmured, but his attention remained held by the patient's still form. "I know what Grandaddy would have said."

"I beg your pardon?"

"My grandfather was a real old-timey country doctor. Covered the better part of three counties by horse and buggy. Tough life. Tough old man." Dr. Meadows grinned. "He would've asked if you'd tried yelling at him to wake up."

"Really, doctor, I don't see how—"

But Dr. Meadows had already stooped down low by the patient's head. He fitted two fingers in his mouth, took a deep breath, and gave an ear-splitting whistle.

The patient opened his eyes, furrowed his brow, turned his head, and asked sleepily, "What in the world did you do that for?"

Dr. Meadows smiled in satisfaction. Dr. Prain's jaw dropped a good three inches as he took an involuntary step backward.

The patient looked around. "Where am I?"

"In the hospital, son," Dr. Meadows replied. "You've had an accident."

The patient scanned the room. "But what am I doing *here*?"

"You've had everybody right worried," Dr. Meadows said. "You've been asleep for quite some time."

"No, I haven't." The patient struggled but could not rise.

"What's the matter with me? And what are these tubes doing attached to my arm?"

"Easy does it, son." Dr. Meadows laid a restraining hand on the patient's chest. "You've been out for four days. How do you feel?"

"I feel fine," he said, looking more worried by the moment. "Where is Bliss?"

"Who?" Dr. Meadows turned and asked. "Was there someone in the van with him?"

"No, he was alone."

"I can't be here," Dan said worriedly, his motions tired and feeble. "Not now."

"But you are here, son. And by the looks of things, you're going to need to stick around a while longer. Let your body have the time to get reacquainted with itself." Dr. Meadows said over his shoulder, "Maybe you ought to have the nurse prepare something to help him relax."

Dr. Prain, speechless, started backing toward the door.

"I don't *want* to relax," the patient said, his voice rising sufficiently to follow the doctor down the hallway. "Where are my swords?"

–NINE–

"You're awake," Bliss said with relief. "Finally."

She retreated farther back into the room's solitary bed, bundled the bedclothes up to her chin, and looked down at Dan. He had slept on the floor between her and the door, his sword at his side.

Dan raised himself up, braced his weight upon one arm, rubbed his face, looked around, and said, "I'm here."

Bliss cocked her head to one side. Tangled locks the color of sun-ripened wheat tumbled over one shoulder. "Where else would you be?"

"I mean, I'm back."

Bliss showed her dimples. "Is that how a knight in your land greets the new day?"

Dan turned to where she was sitting and gazing down on him, and the relief of having been transported back gave him the courage to say, "You are the most beautiful thing that's ever happened to me."

A faint tint of color touched her cheeks. "That is indeed a more gallant greeting."

"It is wonderful to look at you," Dan went on. "I wish

there were some way to tell you how I feel when I'm with you."

"Enough, enough, please," she cried, blushing a bright pink from her ears to the tip of her nose. "Now is neither the time nor the place for such talk as this."

Dan nodded. "I just wanted to tell you."

"Tell me you have, and I shall keep every word locked safely in my heart of hearts until your quest is behind you and we are again together," she promised softly.

Dan slid from his bedding, which consisted of a pair of old quilts laid upon the hardwood floor. The hotel had been full save for this one room, and Bliss had showed relief to know he would be sleeping close at hand.

"The din from below woke me several times in the night," she said. "It seemed as though all the dark knights had gathered to lay waste to our hostel."

"I must have missed it," Dan said, moving behind the dressing screen.

"Yes, I heard your snores and took great comfort from having such an alert watchman nearby."

Once they were dressed and their belongings gathered, they went downstairs. The inn's great room was already bustling. Dan followed the example of those he had seen the night before by carrying his weapons bundled in his left hand. This seemed to be generally accepted as a sign of peace.

Their appearance was greeted with a moment's silence, as it had been the night before. Dan felt all eyes track them to their places, but like Bliss he pretended to pay them no mind.

Just as he was seating himself, Dan spotted a familiar face in the corner. A pair of dark eyes stared malevolently in his direction. Dan felt an idea suddenly take form in his mind, as though gifted from somewhere beyond himself.

"I'll be right back," he said, setting his belongings on the table.

As Dan approached the corner, the man's two comrades rose to their feet, their hands resting on half-drawn swords. Dan showed open palms, approached, and stopped directly in front of the dark-haired man. The man remained seated, flanked by his two accomplices. His eyes blazed with the hatred of one scorned.

"Yesterday you accused me of stealing your pride," Dan said. Although his voice was quiet, in the sudden silence his words carried to the room's farthest reaches. "I still say I didn't do anything except defend myself. But I don't like leaving you to think otherwise."

Dan extended his hand across the table. "So if I took anything of yours, I'm here to give it back."

The man stared up at Dan, uncertainty now in his gaze. Dan willed him to take his hand.

Hesitantly the man raised his own hand, touched it briefly to Dan's, dropped it to the table, and averted his eyes.

"May there be peace between us," Dan said, dropping his arm. "And between all men."

He walked back across the utterly motionless room. Only when he was seated did the murmuring resume.

He was rewarded with a gaze from blue eyes shining like earthbound stars. "If we were elsewhere I would embrace you with all my strength," Bliss said softly.

"Then let's go elsewhere," Dan said. "Right now."

"That was the chivalry of fables," she said, her look so intense it gave him shivers.

"Either that," said a querulous voice behind Dan, "or the young man is a knight schooled in high foolishness."

"Meadows!" Bliss exclaimed, rising from her seat to

rush around and hug a bent old man. "What are you doing here?"

"Looking for you, of course. Wouldn't spend a second in Borderland for any less important a reason." Eyes the color of a winter sky and filled with the light of eternal youth fastened themselves upon Dan. "And I find you escorted by the greatest swordsman in the land, or at least some are speaking thus."

"As well they should," Bliss said, looking fondly upon Dan.

Dan rose slowly to his feet. His brow furrowed as he said, "This is crazy, but I could swear I've seen you before."

The old man squinted, then grinned and said, "Only if my back was turned. For I never forget a face, and yours is one I would have remembered."

"Where, Daniel?" Bliss asked.

"He looks like the guy who woke me up."

Bliss straightened. "But *I* woke you."

"Not this morning. Before."

"What?"

Dan shook his head. "Never mind."

"This is Meadows," Bliss said. "Named such because he spends his time running from one to the next."

"Not any longer," Meadows corrected, his grin as ageless as his gaze. "No longer running, that is."

"Meadows is our greatest herbalist," Bliss explained. "He knows the quality of every green thing. What is useful for which ailment, what is not."

"I am but a student of the Lord of Light's great creation," Meadows corrected, sweeping one hand about. He was little more than skin and bones and sinew, without an ounce of fat upon his sparse frame. "This glorious earth and all the plants that call it home."

"A study worthy of a thousand lifetimes," Dan said, trying to be noble while still wishing for nothing more than to be alone with Bliss.

"One lifetime will do," the old man replied with a chuckle. "Often I wonder if one is not too much."

"Were I to require the services of a healer," Bliss said, "there is none I would wish for save Meadows."

"That is because the greatest healing is done with love, not with medicines," Meadows replied. "And this old man has long loved you from afar."

"Not so old," Bliss said. "And, I hope, not too far away. Not ever."

"Sweet words for one of my years to hear." Meadows winked in Dan's direction. "Let us hope that yon knight will not take exception to these favors."

But Dan was still puzzling over how similar the old man's features were to those of the doctor who had whistled in his ear.

"May I sit with you?" Meadows asked.

"Of course."

"I thank you." Meadows leaned his long hardwood staff against the table and dropped his shoulder-sack to the floor at his feet. When he had seated himself, he asked Dan, "Is it a quest which brings you here?"

"Yes," Bliss replied for him.

"And what, may an old man ask, is that quest?"

"I don't know," Dan replied distractedly.

"He won't tell me either," Bliss said.

Meadows asked, "Where are you headed?"

He shrugged. "You've got me."

"What strange speech this knight has," Meadows said.

"He is from a distant land," Bliss explained. "And he is headed into the valley."

"So." Meadows leaned two hands the color and density

of gnarled tree roots upon the table. "I also am traveling in that direction."

"You?" Bliss stared at him. "But why?"

"Because there are flowers that grow in that valley," Meadows explained, "and no place else on earth."

"How long will you stay?"

"Not a moment longer than necessary," he replied, his eyes still on Dan. "And I would feel far safer traveling in the company of a knight such as yourself."

There was a moment's silence, then Bliss said, "Though I am troubled by the thought of anyone traveling in that direction, if you must go, I would be more at peace knowing that you travel together."

Meadows asked, "Would you be willing to take the road that leads to the lower fields?"

Dan shrugged. "Since I don't know where I'm going, I guess one road's as good as the next."

"Then it is settled." The old man practically leaped to his feet. "Let us be off. My feet long for a path which is not paved, and my nostrils for air which has not been breathed by a thousand other folk."

The path continued unbroken. Wild flowers bloomed. Birds sang. Tree limbs shivered gently in the new breeze. But still Dan knew the moment he crossed the invisible line. It was a border not known by his material senses, yet there was no question. He felt a sudden chill deep in his bones.

He turned around and saw that Bliss had pulled the horse to a stop. Meadows continued on unabated, his pace overbrisk for one carrying his burden of years.

Dan returned to Bliss, and as he did he felt a shiver run through his body, as though a sudden soothing warmth had pushed the cold aside. A warmth so gentle and peaceful that Dan knew it only by its absence. Standing again outside the border, feeling the warmth he had taken for granted until it was gone, Dan knew real fear for the first time since his arrival.

"I can go no farther," Bliss said sadly.

"I understand."

She slipped from the horse's back and said, "I do not have your strength."

He shook his head. "You have the strength of ten of me," he replied truthfully. "But you belong in a world filled with good things and good people, and I have a feeling there isn't much of either beyond this point."

She gazed deep. "I should have known you would see the border."

"Not see," he corrected. "Feel."

"You saw with your heart," she said and smiled at him. "May the Lord of Light guide your footsteps and show you what to do. Know that in my heart I walk alongside you and would shield you with all that I am and all that I have."

"I would give anything," he said softly, "to be anywhere else, so long as it was with you."

"May that time soon come," she said, holding his gaze steady in hers. "You are a true friend, Knight Daniel. All my life I have heard there were people like you. I hoped and dreamed of meeting a gallant knight, but never," she paused to take a shaky breath, "never did I imagine one so filled with goodness."

"The only goodness I have in me," Dan replied, "is what you put there yourself."

Her smile wavered. "Your modesty is astonishing."

"I am a knight only because you called me one," he continued, "and then had confidence in me."

"I do, I do." She sighed. "My heart is full of such confidence. That and more."

"Friend," he agreed, suddenly unable to say more. A longing for more than what was between them left him speechless.

She reached up behind her neck and unclasped a slender chain. Bliss lifted from her bodice a sliver of gold which seemed to capture all light and magnify it, sending it out in all the colors of all the world's rainbows.

"This is my most precious possession," Bliss said quietly. "A gift from Cousteau when I studied the Book's mysteries with him. He says that all is revealed, but I did not have the power of vision to see. He gave me this, which he called the reflection of the light that now rests eternally within my heart."

Her eyes filled with tears, and more. "Know that my heart goes with you, Knight Daniel. I shall walk every step of the way with you."

"I could . . ." Dan began and had to stop. Why, he did not know. He wanted to say, I could turn around and go back with you, but the words were not there. In that moment he knew with painful clarity that his own way lay forward into the unknown.

She understood. "Go swiftly and return with all the speed granted you."

Dan accepted the locket. As he grasped it in his fist, he felt a surge of warmth and light and love bathe his innermost being.

"This is the only badge I shall ever wear," he promised her. "And if ever my path descends into darkness, I know your love will be there to see me through."

"My love," she agreed, her voice barely a whisper. A tear escaped to trace its way down her cheek. "I shall not be complete until you have returned to my side."

Dan raised a single finger, captured the tear, and raised it to his lips. Then he lowered his head and placed his lips upon hers.

When he raised his head, her own face remained upturned, her lips parted, her eyes reluctant to open and release him. Dan found himself captured by the moment, standing and looking down at the upturned face, drinking in the sight of her, knowing he would carry this image with him forever.

Her eyelids fluttered, as though she were rising to wakefulness from the greatest of depths. "Go," she sighed. "Go, my Daniel, so that soon you may return."

Dan turned and began down the path after Meadows, his heart tolling like a cracked bell.

–Ten–

Dan opened his eyes and found himself staring at the biggest, blackest woman he had ever seen.

Her moon-size face was up close to his as she tucked in the edges of his sheet. Her name tag, which was right at eye level, read "Elvira."

When she realized he was awake, she showed him eyes as big as saucers and said, "Why, hello there." Her voice was deeper than Dan's. "How are you feeling?"

"All right." He looked around and sighed. "Am I back in the hospital again?"

"Back again?" Her chuckle was deep and good-natured. She reached up and pressed a button on the wall monitor, saying, "Honey, you haven't budged from this bed for more than five days."

"Five days," Dan murmured, aching for Bliss, unable to face the fear that he might not see her again.

Elvira asked, "Would you like something to drink?"

Dan nodded, allowed a straw to be fitted in his mouth, and drank deeply. "Thank you."

"Don't mention it." She smiled down at him. "You've

had everybody around here wondering if you were ever going to wake up."

The door swung open for a white-coated doctor who said, "What's the—" then saw that Dan's eyes were open. "You again."

Dan shut his eyes and willed himself back.

"No, you don't!" The doctor rushed over and gripped Dan's arm. "Don't you dare drop off."

Reluctantly Dan obeyed.

"That's better." The doctor permitted himself to relax a notch. "I'm Dr. Prain. Can you tell me your name?"

"Dan Simmons."

"And your address?"

Dan gave it to him.

The doctor nodded. "Do you know how you got here?"

"You mean, do I remember the accident? Sure." He found himself staring at the nurse, who hovered around the foot of his bed. There was a look of deep and genuine concern about her face. Dan decided that he liked her.

"Are you in any pain?"

"No."

"No headache, backache, discomfort in your abdomen?"

"Nothing."

"How about your legs?"

"I feel fine."

"Nurse, give me a hand, please." Together they rolled back Dan's bedclothes. "All right. Wriggle your hands and toes. Fine. Can your raise your legs at the knees? How about your arms?"

Dan watched the doctor's expression as he went through the required motions, and wondered why the man seemed disappointed when Dan did as he was asked.

His eyes on Dan, Dr. Prain said to the nurse, "See if Dr. Meadows is still in the building."

"I believe he's next door with the little girl," she replied.

Dr. Prain jerked around. "What's he doing over there?"

"He was in here when I came to change the patient's bedding," the nurse answered. "He said as he left that he was going over to take a look at her."

"Dr. Meadows is examining my patients without me?" Dr. Prain spoke sharply.

Dan watched as the nurse's eyes narrowed, and decided that he would not want her to become angry with him. Not ever.

"I didn't say he was examining," she replied quietly. "He said he just wanted to look in on the sleepers."

"Why wasn't I informed? Oh, never mind." Dr. Prain spun around and left in a huff.

The nurse looked thoughtfully at the door for a long moment, then said to Dan, "I hope you don't mind me referring to you like that. It's what the whole hospital is calling you both. Our two sleepers."

"That's okay," Dan replied. "You say there's a little girl here too?"

"Next door. Except she hasn't woken up. Starts to every hour or so, but then she drifts off again. She's got everybody real worried."

"How old is she?"

"Consuela is nine. She hit her head on a table four days ago and is still out. They're talking about doing exploratory surgery tomorrow. They have to do something, I suppose, but it's a shame. She looks as comfortable as you, just like she's taking a long nap."

The door opened to admit Dr. Prain and another white-coated doctor.

As soon as the second man came into view, Dan's eyes

opened wide. He pointed and shouted, "It *is* you!"

The words stopped Dr. Prain in his tracks. The second man swiveled and scouted behind himself. When he saw nothing he turned back and said, "Yes?"

"You're Meadows!"

"Lower your voice, son." Dr. Meadows approached the bed and peered down with kindly inquisitive eyes. "Now how did you know my name?"

Dan let his head fall back on his pillow. "This is too much."

"I probably said it," Dr. Prain offered. The turn of events was having a remarkably unsettling effect on Dr. Prain. He snapped his fingers. "Now I remember. You were here the last time he woke up. He read your name tag."

"I never wear one," Dr. Meadows said, his eyes not leaving Dan's face. "Son, how did you know my name? Did you hear Dr. Prain use it?"

"That's as good an excuse as any," Dan murmured toward the ceiling.

"I seem to have startled you. Is something the matter? Are you in any pain?"

The fatigue settled over him like a welcoming mist. Dan smiled contentedly and just had time to say, "I'm fine. Everything's fine now. It's time to . . ."

Dr. Prain stepped forward, bent over, peeled back an eyelid, and choked on an expletive. He rose slowly and said, "He's gone again."

Dan sat at the edge of a vast field. An occasional hint of a breeze touched the grassland, sending ripples across an open green sea. Flecks of blooming color dotted the green. Heat flickered in the sunlit air. Birds twittered. Flies buzzed. Butterflies danced from flower to flower.

Dan was positively bored to tears.

The old man wandered about talking to himself. Meadows would take a step, bend down, shake his head, mutter something, and move on. Then he would cry out and pounce upon a poor unsuspecting wild flower or nettle or herb.

There was no one else about. They had not seen another soul since crossing the invisible border that morning. The sun was now gradually westering, and Dan had never known a day that seemed so long.

His eyelids weighed about two tons each.

The only thing keeping him from taking another nap was the memory of what had happened when he stretched out after their lunch of bread and cheese. He remained fearful that if he slept he might not wake up again.

At least, not here.

The old man walked over, dropped his staff and his sack, and eased himself down with much creaking and popping of ancient joints. "Ah, that's better. My feet were beginning to wonder if I would ever let them rest."

A fresh spiciness wafted from the sack. Dan pulled it closer, opened the neck, and sniffed. "That smells great."

"Aye, the body knows what is good for it." Meadows leered. "As does the heart, no?"

Dan found himself reddening. "I guess so."

"Aye, lad. Were I but twenty years younger, I'd give you quite a battle for that maid's affections."

It was Dan's turn to grin. "Twenty years?"

Meadows waved his hand distractedly. "Be that as it may, it appears to these old eyes that you are—"

His observation was cut short by very faint cries upon the wind.

Both Dan and Meadows straightened and strained to hear.

There it was again. Closer now. Then the breeze rustled nearby grasses, and the sound was wafted away.

"Can you tell whence it comes?" The old man struggled to his feet. "I know you will think it is my age, but—"

"It sounds like it's coming from overhead," Dan agreed, scanning the skies.

"Ah, thank goodness. I am not going daft after all."

Dan pointed. "There. What kind of bird is that?"

The old man squinted, then asked, "What on earth is a stork doing in these parts?"

Then the sound was carried to them once more. "Steady, I say, steady! Ooof! I'm not a sack of meal, you know! Wait, there they are! Look, down there. No, not there, you addled skunk with wings. There!"

The bird dipped and swooped, accompanied by a drawn-out, "Aiiieeee!!"

The stork settled with a flapping of its great wings. Immediately a voice said, "Well, for goodness' sake, don't just stand there like stumps. Someone come and untie me!"

Dan approached to find a chocolate-colored bunny tied to the stork's back with a ribbon the color of cornflower eyes. "Napoleon?"

" 'You must go,' she said. 'You're the only one light enough to ride who knows what he looks like.' 'But I don't *want* to go,' I said. 'If bunnies were meant to fly, we'd have feathers. Find a bigger bird and send Eleander. She'd probably love it.' But have you ever tried to argue with Bliss?"

"No," Dan replied, loosening the knot, then picking up the rabbit and setting him on the ground. "Is that better?"

"Ah, earth! Good, sweet earth. And grass! I was wondering if I'd live to nibble again."

Dan remained kneeling beside Napoleon. "So what brings you here?"

"I'll tell you what brought me here." A tiny forepaw

pointed shakily at the stork. "That creature with the heart of an owl brought me, and did its best to scare me to death in the process."

Dan glanced to where Meadows was watching the proceedings from the comfort of a nearby log. "I meant, *why* did you come?"

The rabbit sat upon its forepaws and said solemnly, "Bliss arrived back home to discover that the Book of Light has been stolen."

"What?" Meadows leapt to his feet. "Say it is not so!"

"But it is," Napoleon replied. "A great lone raven, or what traveled in the form of a raven, flew in at yesterday's sunset. The little girl, Consuela, was in the chamber. Cousteau has been instructing her, and she has taken to spending more and more time up there alone."

"All is lost," Meadows murmured. "Without the Book . . ."

"Bliss found Cousteau bedridden and unable to do more than moan. She says that all hope now rests in your hands, and your hands alone."

Dan settled back on his haunches. "Where do I go?"

The rabbit inspected him for a long moment, then replied, "I have told you all I know."

A memory from the hospital set off alarms in his mind. "And Consuela?"

"Scared, sorrowful as are we all. But otherwise all right. She hid beneath a chair when the raven tried to attack her."

"I need you to take a couple of messages back for me. Please."

The bunny gave a long-suffering sigh. "I suppose I might as well."

"The first one is to Consuela. You need to tell her exactly what I say, even if it doesn't make any sense to you." Dan took a breath. "Tell her she is in the hospital back home, in the room next to mine. She hit her head. She has to try and wake up, because if she doesn't they may operate on her."

Napoleon looked up at Dan. "That's it?"

"This is very important."

"You wish me to risk life and limb to deliver that gibberish?"

Dan nodded. "Can you repeat it back to me?"

Doing so put the bunny in a very foul mood. "Yes? And now? There is something more? Perhaps you'd like me to entertain you? Eat a worm?"

"Just tell Bliss," Dan said and then paused, seeing a grin sprout upon the old man's face. He finished in a rush, "Tell her I carry her with me everywhere."

"More gibberish," the rabbit muttered, and looked over to where the stork stood preening itself with utter unconcern. "Oh me, oh my. I suppose there's no use putting it off any longer."

Dan lifted the bunny, settled him on the stork's back, tied the ribbon in place, and asked, "Comfortable?"

"How dare you use that word when I'm about to be scared white," Napoleon replied. "Is that a smirk on your face?"

"Take care, Napoleon."

"I distinctly saw a smirk. Very well, just for that I intend to forget your messages."

"Tell Consuela the only way I know to go home is to fall asleep," Dan replied. "And tell Bliss I miss her."

"More gibberish. Aaaaaah!" The cry came as the stork unfolded its wings and gave a tentative flap.

Dan stepped back as the stork powered up. As it flew away there descended ever fainter cries.

"My heart! My heart isn't up to this! No, no, don't swoop! Don't you dare swoop! Watch out for the tree, you blundering dodo!"

Dan turned back to Meadows and asked, "What do I do now?"

"I have a friend we need to see," Meadows replied, hefting his sack. "Come. It is time to take the unwelcome trail."

– Eleven –

"These old bones," Meadows said, each word pushed out by the jouncing trot, "are far happier with a seat that stays still."

"These young bones too," Dan agreed, but for the moment he was quite happy to put up with the discomfort. He was *riding*. He was riding a *horse*. And bareback to boot.

"It troubles me also," Meadows went on, "that we have seen no one else upon this road. Traffic has been slight since the invasion, but never have I seen it thus."

Meadows had insisted upon their riding. It was essential, he had said, that they arrive before dark. Dan had offered feeble protests as the old man had called and the horse had come trotting over. His objections had grown feebler as he had watched Meadows ask the horse if they could ride up together, as they were now in an urgent hurry. He had stopped talking altogether as the horse had first nodded, then sort of half knelt so that Meadows could easily slip onto its back.

Dan had then clambered aboard and would have fallen off the other side had the horse not shifted its balance and offered a protruding flank for leverage. Before he realized what he was doing, Dan thanked the horse, who replied with a gentle snort and started trotting in the direction Meadows pointed out.

Now that Dan was fairly certain the horse would not let him fall off, he was thoroughly enjoying the experience. He had had no idea that sitting upon a horse would make him feel so *high*. What Meadows said was true—the gait jounced him quite severely. At the same time, he sensed that the horse was keeping his back as stable as possible for them.

As dusk fell, they spotted over the treetops a tower pennant snapping in the breeze. Dan felt Meadows stiffen in front of him.

"There is something I must tell you," he said. "If we are to share this danger, then you should know how entry is possible."

"I'm all ears."

"Life has become more complicated since the Dark King's arrival," Meadows continued. "At Cousteau's request, I have become a gatherer of tidings."

"A spy," Dan said, grinning at the back of the old man's head.

Meadows shrugged. "In many of the conquered residences we have managed to persuade one loyal to us to remain. My herbs are required by all, good and bad alike. In exchange for the freedom to travel when and where I wish, I am sometimes able to assemble information."

"So you have a friend here at court," Dan finished for him. "I like it."

"Not exactly at court," Meadows corrected. "In truth, she is the head cook and the only resident healer."

The structure that grew from the gloaming was a castle in the true sense of the word. It crowned the top of a fair-sized hill and was ringed by a succession of three high battlements. Outside the third rested a large moat. The castle itself possessed great windows and lofty archways and turrets galore. In the final light of day, it was about the most impressive thing Dan had ever seen.

They halted upon reaching the final grove of trees. Ahead of them, open fields swept up to the moat and the first ramparts.

"We must leave your steed here," Meadows said, patting the horse's flank. "To arrive upon a mount would give rise to unwanted questions."

"Fine with me." Dan slid from the horse, then helped ease his companion to the ground. As Meadows tottered about, rubbing his back and loosening his joints, Dan patted the horse's flank and said, "Thanks."

The horse snorted, for all the world as though it understood him perfectly.

"Uh," Dan started, feeling more than a little foolish talking to a horse, "it'd be best if you'd stay as close to the road as you can without being seen. I guess there's a chance we'll be coming out of here at a run."

"The guards are arriving to raise the drawbridge," Meadows hissed. "We must hurry."

Dan shouldered his bow, hefted the old man's bulky sack, watched the horse disappear into the surrounding forest, and said, "Let's do it."

Their arrival caused mild consternation among the guards. There was a brief gathering, then a voice boomed out, "Halt! Who goes there?"

"And do you not even know your own herbalist anymore?" Meadows replied, giving his voice a more querulous tone than normal. "Is that not the captain of the guard I treated just two seasons ago for a wound that would not heal?"

"Meadows?" The burly guard grasped a torch from one

of his fellows and held it aloft. "Is that you?"

"It is indeed, traveling with a young friend who is armed against the evils that might befall an old man in these uncertain times." Meadows drew up to the gathered soldiers and stopped, puffing from the climb. "Is there not a bed and perhaps a crust of bread for two tired travelers?"

The guard glanced worriedly behind him. "This is not a good time, Meadows. The count—"

A voice from behind cut him off with, "Who goes there, Captain? Is it perhaps someone traveling without the necessary permits?"

The captain of the guard snapped to attention, as did all his men. "I was just coming to that, my lord."

"Then it is good that I arrived when I did, is it not?" A tallish figure in fur-trimmed robes strode forth, his way lighted by four liveried servants bearing lanterns.

"Indeed so, my lord," the captain said, casting a fretful glance in Meadows' direction.

Dan's eyes widened as the flickering light illuminated the count's frowning countenance. It was the face of the second doctor.

He hid his surprise by following Meadows' example and bowing deep.

The count stopped a pace away from them and asked in his most officious manner, "Whom do we have here?"

"The herbalist, my lord. Meadows."

The count sniffed. "And this other person?"

"His retainer, my lord. I do not know his name."

"Well, ask him," the man snapped impatiently.

"Very good, my lord." The captain swiveled about and barked, "Count Prain demands that you give your name."

"Dan. Daniel," Dan replied, still bowing, as was Meadows.

"Well, which is it?" The voice was impatient, cold, impersonal. "A person cannot possess two names. It is not allowed. It is written in the book of laws, I am sure, although I cannot recall where just at the moment." He turned to one of his henchmen and demanded, "I am right, am I not? A person is permitted but one name, is that not correct?"

"It is indeed just as the illustrious count has stated," the man answered, bowing as he did so. "One name per person."

"There, you see? I knew I was right. Now then," he said, turning back, "which is your name? Dan or Daniel?"

"Daniel," he replied, then for good measure added, "my lord."

The count sniffed and said, "Make a note of that."

"Yes, my lord."

"And your traveling papers?"

"I don't have any," Dan said, for some reason suddenly feeling very queasy.

"What?" The count looked affronted. "Was it not announced throughout the kingdom last week that anyone found upon the open road without the proper authority would be dealt with most harshly? Did that order not go out?"

"Indeed it did, Most Eminent One," the captain intoned. "Just as you so ordered."

"Of course it did. And now what do we have but two travelers who arrive far later than the permitted hour, and without a paper between them." The news appeared to please the count no end.

"You will remember me, of course, Your Honor," Meadows said, his voice timorous, his body twisted like an arthritic pretzel about his walking stick. "I treated you for those awful pains in the belly, why, it wasn't three moons ago. Then and there you said that no one else in the kingdom had been able to help you. You told me with your own words that had it not been for me—"

"Of course, of course." A note of faltering hesitation appeared in the count's eyes, then as quickly disappeared. "I just remembered. I issued special traveling papers to you, Meadows. They were written up and set aside for your arrival." He glanced at his aide and said sharply, "Is that not so?"

"Indeed it is exactly as you stated, Most Exalted One."

The count turned back with a flourish. "There, you see?"

Again Meadows bowed deep. "I am indeed grateful for Your Honor's bountiful mercy. And for my retainer?"

The count inspected Dan with a lofty nose. "I recall nothing that was stated about any retainer. Am I not correct?"

"It is exactly as you state, O Benevolent One. There was nothing in regards to any retainer."

"Of course not. Why should you have any need for a retainer in this kingdom? Our byways are perfectly safe, are they not, Captain?"

"Safe as any man can make them, my lord."

"Exactly." The gaze rested upon Dan with a dangerous gleam. "Besides, I have received new orders from the Tower of Abandon, have I not?"

"Just this afternoon, O Mighty One."

Beside him, Dan noticed Meadows suppress a nervous shiver.

"And it required of me to locate several suitable subjects, did it not?"

"Of good health, O Potent One," the captain agreed.

"Yes. And this paperless person appears to be in good health, does he not?" The count signaled to the captain. Before Dan could react, several pairs of very strong arms held him in a viselike grip.

"Search him carefully from head to toe," the count said,

turning away, his servants retreating like well-trained dogs. "Then cast him into the dungeon."

Dan found himself so trapped by discomfort and despair that he was unable to sleep. The night seemed endless. Even when day arrived, his night continued. He knew it was day only because of the hammering and shouting and clattering that arose outside his cell door. It continued unabated for hour after hour after hour. Dan drifted in and out of an exhausted stupor, willing himself to sleep, yet unable to do so.

The cell's only illumination came from a flickering lantern, so filthy as to release barely a grudging glow. The cell was all of rough stone, dank to the touch, fetid with the years of memories and fear and pain. The door was stout and oaken and permanently barred. Food and water were passed through a small opening at its base, covered with a thick leather sheet so as to bar further light. The one time Dan lay on his belly, pushed the cover aside, and tried to look out, his fingers were rapped so hard he thought they had been broken.

The dark chamber sucked away Dan's hope, leaving him more afraid than he had ever been in his life. He ached with loneliness and with the fear of knowing no release. He tried to imagine Meadows pleading for his freedom or riding back for reinforcements, but as the hours dragged by Dan came to see all such longing as futile.

A chain ran from his ankle to an iron plate bolted to one side wall. Dan had just enough play to reach for whatever slop was shoved through the door slit. He could touch the cell's far wall by lying down and extending one hand out as far as he could reach. A second chain extended from that wall, but it was empty.

Concrete pallets ran along both side walls. Dan lived upon the one he could reach. He sat there, ate there, sprawled there, and worried how and when it might all end.

When the din finally died down outside his door, he was so exhausted that he knew sleep would not be long in coming. He lay down with a long sigh of relief, hoping he would awaken in the hospital. Freed from the dungeon. Able to pass on a message through Consuela. Able to eat a decent meal, even if it wouldn't fill his belly on the other side. Above all, able to know a few moments of light and freedom.

Instead, Dan slept like a log.

He awoke with a groan from having spent the night on a concrete slab with his arm for a pillow. His entire body was one big ache. When he realized he had not been anywhere but asleep, he groaned a second time, louder than the first.

As he sipped the dregs from his wooden water pail, doom beat its relentless beat in time to his heart. It occurred to him that his spirit was locked in here as well. The air of hopelessness was so strong, his spirit was chained as effectively as his body. These cold stone walls would hold him trapped and helpless for the rest of his days.

Then a key turned in the lock, and Dan leapt to his feet. The door creaked loudly on its hinges.

"Ah, yes, there you are." Count Prain stepped in, flanked by two burly guards. He peered about the cell in a fussy manner. "Everything appears to be in order. You are keeping well, I assume."

Dan eased himself back down upon the stone slab. "Not particularly."

"Yes, well, you are in a dungeon, of course. A bit of discomfort is to be expected. Other than that, everything is orderly? Correct? Under control?"

"Everything is just dandy. When do I get out?"

"Oh, you never get out." The count raised the sheaf of papers he was holding. "These forms oblige me to run some tests on you. They will add to your discomfort, of course, but that can't be helped."

"What kind of tests?" Dan asked suspiciously.

"I am instructed by the Tower of Abandon to make a study and report back in detail." He flipped over several pages. "Yes, here it is. I am to take healthy individuals—" He looked up and demanded, "I presume that you are healthy?"

"Reasonably."

"Subject reports himself to be reasonably healthy," the count said, scribbling busily. "And you are, as we can both see, an individual."

"What sort of tests?" Dan repeated.

The count looked up from his page. "Oh, yes. I am instructed to see how much pain these healthy subjects can take."

Dan felt the terror-chill grip his belly. "And then?"

The count looked surprised. "Why, and then you die, of course." He waved the papers before him. "It's all laid out precisely here in black and white, as good orders always are. I shall need to stop the proceedings from time to time and ask you questions such as, have you ever felt anything this horrid, have you ever imagined anything could be this bad, or do you think it could possibly be any worse. That sort of thing."

Dan leaned back against the wall. Cold and clammy fingers gripped his chest so hard he could not speak. The dark walls appeared to gloat at him.

"Orders are orders, you know." When Dan said nothing, the count let the pages fall and went on, "It will take us some time to prepare everything as we have been instructed. I suppose you have heard my servants working. Yes, of course you have. We are marching right along, in an orderly fashion, of course. We should be ready to begin by tomorrow afternoon or the morning after at the very latest. Until then, I shall expect you to remain as you are now. Your state of health has been noted, and my records must be kept accurate."

The count stepped back, the guards followed, and the door was slammed shut.

The utter hopelessness of his situation beat down upon him in waves. When he could bear no more, Dan lowered his head to his knees and wept for the first time since he was a child. He cried, and knew the loneliest moment that had ever been.

He was as utterly broken in spirit as his body would be upon the morrow. With each beat of his heart, Dan felt the pain of yet another small death.

And when he could weep no more, he curled into a tight little ball upon the unyielding slab and shivered himself to sleep.

–Twelve–

This time, Dan somehow managed to stay alert through the transition. At least, that is, for part of it.

Although he knew there was more to the journey, and had seen it often enough for it to seem familiar, all he could clearly remember afterward was passing over the waterfall. The torrent, he knew as soon as he saw it, was made from the tears of all the world's sad people. Dan looked down from his great soaring height and knew that somewhere down there flowed his tears as well. Knew too that somehow the endlessly spilling waterfall united him with all people, of all time, of all lands. For who among men had lived on earth and not known a time of sadness?

Reluctantly he pulled his gaze away and realized that his way was lighted by a brilliant orb overhead. He suddenly became aware that the great warming light was both the sun and more, for it warmed his heart as well as his body. Its touch reached to the deepest part of his being, and healed and soothed. Its peace was gentle, yet overwhelming. And Dan knew that somehow this new awareness was going to change his life forever.

Then he awoke.

———

Dan lay in starched white comfort. Sunlight poured through his window, casting a golden pillar across the foot of his bed. He lay in the splendor of release, too happy at being out of the dungeon to pay much mind either to his unmoving limbs or to the lonely thought that he would soon be forced to return. For the moment, it was enough to be where he was.

The knock at his door sounded overloud in the empty room and shattered Dan's isolation. The latch turned. An old man's smiling face poked through.

"Morning," the man called. "Mind if I come in?"

Dan was so shocked that he could not speak, only shake his head.

It was Cousteau.

"Thanks, thanks. Won't be but a moment." The visitor had a canvas satchel cast over one shoulder. "Just wanted to drop something by. This hospital has been built since my last visit to the area."

Dan asked shakily, "Is your name Cousteau?"

The old man's eyes widened. "Now how on earth did you know that?"

Dan shook his head. "Unbelievable."

"I'll say. We haven't met before, have we?"

"I'm not sure."

"Well, the world's sure got some funny turns to it."

"You said it," Dan agreed.

"Yessir, my pappy was from down New Orleans way," the old man said cheerily. "He was half Cajun. His daddy's daddy was pure French. That's where the name comes from. Guess one of the nurses musta told you I was coming. What's your name, son?"

"Dan." Then for some reason he corrected himself. "Daniel."

"Now that's a name I've always been partial to. Always liked what it stood for. Fellow who can keep hold of his faith in the midst of a lions' den is somebody to look up to, wouldn't you say?" The old man rummaged through his satchel. "What they got you in for?"

"I've been sleeping a lot, sort of," Dan said, still amazed to see the old man's face here. "And I'm having a little trouble walking."

"Aw, hey, that's tough." Cousteau hefted a packet from his satchel.

As it came into view, Dan felt as well as saw what it was and could not help but cry, "The Book of Light!"

"What's that?"

Dan made a vast effort and reached out his hand. "May I have that, please?"

Cousteau beamed as though Dan had paid him the greatest possible compliment. "Why, sure," he said. "It's what brings me around and keeps me going. Hoping that folks here and there might like to take a look at the Truth." He handed it over. "What did you call it?"

"The Book of Light," Dan said softly, accepting the Bible and settling it into his lap. He opened the cover, and felt as well as saw the light and the love stream from the page.

"Never heard it called that before," Cousteau said and chuckled. "But I suppose it's as good a name as any. Says in there that God is light and the Lord of all. If the Word is the spoken truth, then I suppose it must contain all that God is—light and love and everything else."

Dan raised his eyes. "Why are you here?"

"I just told you," the old man replied. "To spread the truth. Pass out these Bibles. Didn't the nurse tell you that?"

"I guess she forgot," Dan replied.

"I've covered this region for nigh on forty years. Been getting harder, though, to make it around. I heard they'd opened this hospital a while back. Been trying to get up this way, but these old legs don't move as fast as they used to." Cousteau smiled at Dan. "You spend much time in the Book, son?"

In the Book. Dan shook his head. "Not as much as maybe I should."

"Wouldn't do you any harm to take a look at the story that carries your name. Daniel was a man who saw visions, but he didn't let those visions get in the way of doing a man's work. He stood by his people in their hour of need and rose high in the ranks of a world that was not his own. That's a nice combination, it seems to me. Feet on the earth and head in the clouds." The old man offered Dan his hand. "Well, just wanted to stop by and give you this. Wish you all the best, son."

"Thanks," Dan replied. "Would you mind passing a message on to the little girl in the next room?"

"Room 237, that right?"

"Yes."

"Yeah, they told me a sweet little girl is staying in that room. Sorry, son, I just came from that way. She's not there."

"She's not?" Dan felt his hopes dashed.

"Nope. Her bedcovers were folded back, and the room was empty. Can I tell the nurse something for you?"

"No," he said sadly. "I guess not."

A thought seemed to strike the man just as he was turning away. "Would you care to pray with me before I go?" he asked.

Dan nodded slowly.

Cousteau pulled over a hard-backed chair and seated himself. "If you're new at this, I'll be happy to say the words myself."

"Thank you," Dan mumbled.

The old man bowed his head and opened his prayer with the words, "O dear Lord Jesus . . ."

And that was all that Dan could hear. For from then on his heart was speaking too loudly. He saw the bonding of Light between them grow and strengthen. He saw the Light emanating from the page in his lap reach out to envelop the room. He felt the Spirit move with a power that overwhelmed him. And he knew that here was the answer. The one, true, everlasting answer. Beyond words, beyond reason, beyond time and space. The single eternal answer, complete in and of itself.

And for that brief instant, as the fatigue wrapped itself back around his form, Dan knew that somehow, some way, the peace was here to stay.

The head nurse was a big woman, with skin the color of polished ebony. She was named Elvira, and she ruled her ward like a benevolent dictator. Elvira had not yet made up her mind about Dr. Prain. There was too much mind about this man, she was beginning to believe, and far too little heart. He acted as though his charts and his papers and his forms and his orderliness were more important than his patients. As though the people were here to serve the forms, rather than the other way around.

She also disliked the way he hovered around the nurses' station, checking charts and inspecting corners, for all the world like some fussy old maid who was about to take out a white glove and trace her finger around hidden edges for dust. He had the habit of pursing his lips and humming tunelessly as he looked around, ignoring everyone there, sort of frowning in a distracted air and giving everybody nervous fits.

She had taken to marching up to him, shoving her ample chest up within inches of his sparse frame and inquiring in a booming no-nonsense voice if there were anything she could do for him. It was usually enough to get the doctor moving on down the hall.

Today Elvira was held at the nurses' station long after she should have been off preparing the patients for dinner. But Dr. Prain ignored her growing impatience. He studied each of her charts in turn, barking out questions that did not need to be asked, bringing her to a slow boil.

"And what's this?" he said sharply. "Who authorized this increase in medication?"

"Dr. Meadows," she drawled. "You remember him? The hospital's chief doctor? Your boss? See that little signature there where it says 'by the authority of'?"

"Hmph." He slapped the metal file cover shut and reached for another. Elvira did not bother to mask her exasperated sigh.

The old man chose that moment to hobble around the corner and into view. "Many thanks, Elvira. Sure do appreciate you letting me stop by."

She smiled for the first time since Dr. Prain had come on duty. "Surely is nice to see you over this way again, Mr. Cousteau. Yessir, it surely is."

"Shoulda been here two months ago," he said, "but I've been having a little trouble getting around."

"Maybe we oughtta find you a bed," Elvira offered. "See if we can find out what's ailing you."

"I can tell you that right off," Mr. Cousteau said. "I'm old, and I'm getting older."

Her smile broadened. "That's just about the clearest diagnosis I've heard around here in days."

"Well, I'm glad to see you're settling in. These folks are sure lucky to have somebody as highly qualified as you working here." The old man gave Dr. Prain a kindly nod and shuffled off.

Dr. Prain had watched the exchange with a steadily deepening frown.

"You take care now," Elvira called, ignoring the doctor's disapproval.

"May the good Lord bless you and your work," the old man replied. He pushed open the door and was gone.

Dr. Prain demanded sharply, "Who was that?"

Elvira's eyes remained on the doors as she replied, "Mr. Cousteau. He brings Bibles. I saw him from time to time at the hospital where I used to work."

"He was distributing Bibles here?"

Something in the doctor's tone of voice caused her to turn and stare at him. Hard. "Yes," she replied firmly.

"Under whose authority?" he snapped.

"Mine," Elvira said, her eyes narrowing.

The angry gaze was too much for Dr. Prain. He set down the file and announced, "I have more important things to do than talk with you about such nonsense." He moved out of the nurses' station. When he was at a safer distance, he went on, "Just remember that when I'm on duty, the authority on this ward rests with me."

Elvira's gaze remained narrowed as she watched the doctor walk down the hall. She was getting closer every minute to a decision about that doctor.

– Thirteen –

Dan rolled over on his stone pallet, drawn up toward consciousness by the thread of something that had woven itself into his dream. He rolled over, groaned as his body complained, opened his eyes, and gradually brought the dungeon into focus.

There on the floor below him stood Napoleon.

"It took you long enough," the bunny said.

Dan sat up as fast as his aching body would allow. "What are you doing here?"

"Staying two hops away from the soup pot," Napoleon snapped. "Being dressed in doll's clothes. Sitting in a chair so hard it's mashed my tail flat, while an obnoxious little girl who would be locked up for cruelty to bunnies if her father did not happen to be a count pretends to pour me tea. Tea!"

Dan gave his face a hard rub and decided now was not the time to smile. "The count's daughter made you her pet?"

The tiny chocolate-colored bunny sniffed an affirmative. "And a cook as big as a mountain hovers in the background, waiting for the horrid little girl to turn around so she can whisk me off to the pantry and relieve me of my pelt."

"Where is Meadows?"

"I haven't the faintest idea. All I know is that yesterday evening your horse appeared all by itself, stamping and pawing the earth, then rising up on its hind legs and neighing so loudly I thought my eardrums would burst." The bunny gave an exasperated snort. "You can guess what happened then."

"Bliss told you to come," Dan surmised.

"With Eleander standing right there beside me, smirking and saying how much she would miss me. Why does it always have to be me, I ask you. Can you imagine anything sillier than a bunny being sent to the rescue of a knight on the back of a horse?"

"At least it wasn't another trip by stork," Dan pointed out.

"Not much better, let me tell you. From where I sit, the back of a horse is far too high for comfort or safety. And the bouncing nearly pushed my stuffing out."

Dan gave his nose a good rub until he had his grin under control. "Well, I'm really glad you came. And grateful."

The genuine feeling behind his words caught Napoleon off guard. The bunny rubbed his face with his little forepaws, pushing his ears down flat and then letting them spring up again. "You're just saying that to be polite."

"No, really, I mean every word," Dan assured him. "You can't imagine how lonely I've been."

The tiny rabbit took a look around the cell and said quietly, "Yes, I can."

"I feel a hundred percent better just having you to talk with," Dan went on. Then he had an idea. He reached down and said, "Here, let me show you something."

"Don't you dare," Napoleon snapped.

"I'm not going to hurt you," Dan said, sliding down onto the floor beside the bunny. "Come over here for a minute."

"What for?" the bunny demanded suspiciously.

"Look, if you don't like it, I promise I'll stop."

The bunny took a tentative hop closer. "Promise?"

"Just come here a second," Dan said, beckoning with his fingers.

Napoleon hopped within reach but remained poised for flight. "Okay, I'm here. So what is it?"

Dan reached down, and with one finger gently rubbed the space between the bunny's chocolate-colored ears. "How's that?"

A little shudder of pleasure ran through the minute form. "All right, I suppose."

Dan lengthened his stroke by a half inch, so that it continued down across the bunny's forehead. "And that?"

Suddenly Napoleon was having trouble keeping his eyes open. He murmured, "Where did you learn to do this?"

"My sister used to have a rabbit that could have been your twin. Except it didn't talk." Dan let his finger trace a path down over Napoleon's back and ribs to the soft spot behind the forepaws. He nudged with one knuckle, and the bunny flopped over without protest.

"You like that, do you?" Dan scratched the soft furry underbelly and allowed his grin to escape as Napoleon's back legs began to kick in reflexive pleasure.

"Just a bit higher, ah, yes, that's it." Napoleon's voice drifted off as Dan found the spot just beneath his chin.

Dan continued his rubbing for a few minutes longer, then stopped and leaned back. The tiny rabbit was a long time coming to. Finally he rolled over and heaved as great a sigh as such a tiny bunny was capable of. "That was magnificent."

"Glad you liked it," Dan said. "Can we be friends now?"

"You give a bunny-rub even better than Bliss, you know." Napoleon's voice was still languid, as though reluctantly waking from a very pleasant dream. "You know when I decided there might be something more to you than I first thought?"

"I never knew you did."

"Oh, yes." Napoleon gave a second sigh, shook himself briskly, and sat upright. "It was back in the field. Do you remember?"

"The day you arrived on the stork? I'll never forget it as long as I live."

"When I told you that the Book had been stolen," Napoleon went on, "your first reaction was, where do I go? Not, all is lost, as Meadows said and the rest of us thought. Just, what do I do now?" The rabbit eyed him calmly. "I began to think then that perhaps Bliss was right. That there was more to you than met the eye."

"I guess we can all make mistakes in judging too fast. People and bunnies alike." He stuck out his hand. "Pals?"

"Pals," Napoleon agreed, allowing Dan to take his forepaw and give it a diminutive shake. "Now the question is, how do we get you out of here?"

"Whatever it is, it has to be done before the castle wakes up," Dan replied. "Tomorrow they crank up whatever it is they've been building out there."

"Be glad you haven't seen it." Napoleon shuddered. "I'll have nightmares for weeks."

"I'd like to have weeks to have nightmares in," Dan said.

"I saw keys hanging on a wall," Napoleon said. "But they were too high for me to reach."

"Meadows mentioned he had a friend here," Dan recalled. "The cook or the healer, or maybe it was both."

"The cook!" squeaked the tiny bunny. "Was she black as night, with a hundred teeth like great fangs?"

"I don't recall him saying—"

"Is she larger than Cousteau's house? Does she have hands bigger than the pots she uses for frying little bunnies?" Napoleon tottered over on his side. "The cook, the cook. Oh, oh, oh. Of all the people in all the world, he wants me to go wake up the cook."

"That's okay, Napoleon," Dan said.

"Help me up," Napoleon said, in an utterly resigned voice. "The cook. Oh me, oh my. She probably has a book called One Hundred and One Ways to Stew a Bunny."

"You really don't have to," Dan repeated, lifting the little form back onto his hind feet.

"The cook," Napoleon sighed, hopping listlessly toward the opening at the bottom of the door. "I probably won't even have time to speak. She sleeps in a chamber beside the pantry, you know, close to all her pots. The count's daughter took me down for morning milk, and this great dark mound was there snoring in a bed as big as a ship. She'll probably wake up and see me and pop me into the oven straight away. Bunny and eggs for breakfast."

Napoleon nosed the leather hanging, stopped, turned around, and said hopelessly, "You're sure he said it was the cook?"

"That's what I remember."

"Oh, oh, oh," Napoleon moaned, pushing through the portal and hopping away. The last thing Dan heard was, "She probably has a special knife for skinning poor helpless bunnies. I wonder if she sleeps with it at her side."

–Fourteen–

Napoleon was gone a very long time. So long Dan began having fleeting visions of the poor rabbit's demise at the hands of a vast and endlessly hungry cook. His new little friend, now strung from a spit and hung over a slow fire—

A key rasped in the lock, and all Dan's world became focused upon the sound.

The door creaked as it opened, and a voice hissed at it to be silent. Dan furrowed his brow. He seemed to have heard that voice somewhere before.

"Well, don't just sit there like an idiot," Napoleon said crossly. "Are you coming or not?"

A vast black face, as big as the moon, squinted into the cell's darkness and asked in a familiar voice, "Is it true what the little one says? Are you indeed a friend of Meadows?"

"Little one," Napoleon muttered. "Hmpf."

Dan answered with a question of his own. "Elvira?"

The great woman backed off a step. "How do you know my name? Did Meadows entrust you with it, or are you empowered by the Dark King?"

"Oh, don't be daft, woman," Napoleon snapped. "If he had anything to do with the dark power, do you think he'd be sitting down here awaiting a fate worse than death?"

Elvira collected herself, looked down at the bunny by her feet, and mused, "Such a mouth on one so small."

"Oh, stuff and nonsense." Napoleon swung toward Dan and demanded, "Well? Are you coming out, or would you prefer for us to come in and join you?"

"There is the small matter," Dan replied, raising his leg, "of my chain."

The rabbit succeeded in making himself even smaller. "Oh, er, a thousand pardons."

Elvira stepped forward. "My mind quakes at the risk I am taking," she said, her hands trembling so hard she had difficulty fitting the key in the ankle brace.

Dan asked, "Are there any guards?"

"Just one, enough for just one prisoner," Elvira replied. The key slid home. "And he sleeps."

"You should have seen her," Napoleon exclaimed. He swept a forepaw in as wide an arc as his tiny length would permit. "Pow! She wielded her skillet like a broadsword."

"Thanks," Dan said, and rubbed the soreness as the anklet fell free. "I'm the only prisoner?"

"All others were sent three days ago to the Tower of Abandon." With the speaking of those final words, a vast tremor coursed through the cook's large frame.

"Please let's not talk about that just now," Napoleon protested. "One fright at a time is already more than this bunny can bear."

"We must fly like the wind," Elvira said, turning for the door.

"Wait," Dan said, rising to his feet. "Where is the Book of Light?"

"Did I not say he was a great knight?" the bunny proclaimed proudly. "Either that or infinitely stupid, I have trouble deciding. He is still in his prison cell, and already he asks of his quest."

"Of that I know nothing," Elvira replied. "Only that all prisoners and all war booty and many of the count's best soldiers have been gathered and sent to the Tower, by order of the Dark King."

Dan stumbled forth, passed through the doorway, and leaned against the wall. His chest heaved, devouring the flavor of freedom. Whatever happened, he would not return to that cell.

Finally he asked, "How do we get out?"

"First we get Meadows," Napoleon replied.

"Meadows?" Dan wished for a sword. "He's here?"

"Locked in the tallest turret, with guards strung throughout the halls between here and there," Elvira moaned. "Truly I love that old man, but to go for him is to go to our deaths."

"I thought—" Dan began, then had to stop. His attention was captured by the fantastic array of torture implements gathered in the center of the chamber.

"The count decided he would be better off holding the healer and bartering his services," Elvira explained. "He is held as an 'honored guest' in the turret, not a prisoner in the dungeon, so it was not necessary to send him onwards."

"What we need," Dan muttered, his anger rising at the sight before his eyes, "is a diversion."

"I'm sure I don't know what that means," Napoleon said worriedly. "Is that another word for getting us into more trouble than we're already in?"

Dan pointed to four giant bowl-shaped vessels of beaten iron. They were set upon high three-legged stands, under which were placed the kindling for fires. "I don't suppose they contain oil, by any chance?"

"Oil, tar, pitch, and acid," Elvira said, sadly shaking her

great head. "Such trouble they go to for the causing of pain."

"Bingo," Dan said.

"I don't know that word either," Napoleon said. "And I'm quite positive I won't like learning about it."

Dan bent over, picked up the rabbit, and said, "I think you'll be more comfortable in my pocket for the duration."

Napoleon allowed himself to be settled into the largest of Dan's vest pockets before asking, "The duration of what?"

Dan patted his pocket. "Comfy?"

"I distinctly recall the last time you asked me that, and I don't think this will be any more pleasant."

"What is the little one talking about?" Elvira said worriedly.

"Good woman," Napoleon snapped from his snug perch, "I will thank you to stop calling me that."

"Come give me a hand," Dan said, rushing toward the first vat. He positioned himself under it, pushed, felt it tip slightly. "We'll have to rock it."

"Whatever for?" Napoleon said, near panic.

Elvira joined him, her eyes suddenly aglow. "Long have I wished for a good way to bid this sad place farewell."

"Let's just hope it works," Dan said.

"Hope *what* works?" Napoleon demanded.

"Destroy them with the fruits of their own labor," Elvira said, putting her great might into the effort. "Oh, I do so like the sound of that."

"Would somebody be so kind," Napoleon said, "as to tell me what on earth is going on?"

"Almost got it," Dan huffed. "On three, now, one, two, *three*."

The bowl teetered, tottered, and spilled over with a resounding clang.

"Oh, how utterly marvelous," the bunny announced. "Now let's see, what else can we do to make some more noise?"

"One more should do it," Dan said, racing with Elvira to the next vat. "Rock, rock, yes, okay, now on three. One, two, *three.*"

This time the clang resounded up and down the chamber.

"I am rendered positively speechless," Napoleon announced. "I thought the idea was to find Meadows and escape. Obviously I was mistaken. I am quite sure we can find a nice loud bell to ring somewhere, in case we haven't yet awakened the *entire blooming castle!*"

"Pretty noisy for a speechless bunny," Dan said around his grin. He then asked Elvira, "You didn't happen to see a sword lying about, did you?"

"Only the one strapped to the soldier who is also lying about," Elvira replied, her own grin displaying what appeared to be twice the customary number of teeth.

"That'll have to do." Dan raced for the stairs, with Elvira close on his heels. For such a vast woman, she was remarkably light on her feet.

The guard was still out cold. Dan slid the soldier's sword free, unleashed his knife, and asked, "Would you care for one of these?"

Elvira lifted her skillet from the stair beside the inert guard and replied, "You are kind, but my hand feels most comfortable fitted around this."

"Right." Dan set down the blades, scaled the wall by embracing the corner column, and lifted the torch from its holder. When he landed on the stairs he said, "Let's hope one of those vats holds something inflammable," and then tossed the torch in a high overhead arc.

He was rewarded with a most satisfactory *WHOOMPF.*

Had they moved any slower, the flames would have singed more than just their eyebrows.

They raced up the stairs, Elvira dragging the groaning guard like a sack of feathers, the smoke billowing up strong behind them. They paused at the top landing, where the stairs opened into a peaked antechamber, to deposit the guard. Voices were already crying out from two of the openings, so they chose the third.

Up another set of stairs, then they stopped to catch their breath and listen for possible pursuit. Dan bent over his pocket and whispered, "Are you all right?"

"Other than feeling distinctly charbroiled," Napoleon replied, "I suppose I can't complain."

Dan turned to Elvira and asked, "Where are we?"

"At the entrance to the west wing," she replied, her words coming in time to her heaving chest. She pointed down along the hallway. "But Meadows is locked in the central turret. How we can get there is a mystery."

"All we need," Dan replied, "is for one of those other vats to—"

His sentence was ended by the solid stone floor shaking mightily under their feet. From the passageway through which they had just come rose the roar of a great angry beast.

"Bingo!" Dan said.

"I am beginning to revise my feelings about that word," Napoleon observed.

"That should have gotten just about everybody's attention," Dan said.

The door behind Dan clicked. Dan instinctively ducked into the shadows. The door was flung aside, to boom resoundingly on the side wall. A soldier's angry voice yelled, "What's going on here?"

Elvira diverted his attention by starting a dance that

had her dress blooming out like a great ship under full sail. "I don't know, O Mighty Sergeant, I'm just a helpless cook, and I was asleep, and then the sky split apart, and the floor heaved and fire and smoke, and oh, my, what's a poor cook to do? Help, help, help!"

"Down the stairs, men!" the sergeant shouted. A number of guards clattered past, weapons at the ready. The guard-sergeant was about to follow, when it occurred to him that something was amiss. He wheeled about and stared at Dan. "Aren't you—"

The query was cut short by Elvira's skillet landing on the side of his helmet with a sound like the gong of time. The guard slumped to the floor.

Dan looked at the man slumbering at his feet and said, "Maybe they should start distributing skillets to all warriors."

"It takes great skill and balance," Elvira said, "and more force than most folk have."

"You've got the swing of a pro," Dan assured her. "Just keep a healthy distance between that weapon of yours and my head, okay?"

"It did have a satisfying ring to it, did it not?" She looked down at the guard with immense satisfaction. "Long have I wanted to give that one something to remember."

"Ahem," Napoleon interrupted. "If this back-patting session is quite through, I seem to remember a rather urgent matter."

"The bunny's got a point," Dan agreed.

Elvira stepped to the door, peered down the long hall, and said, "All noise appears to be below us now."

"Let's move out," Dan said. "Lead the way."

They hastened along a bewildering series of passageways and winding staircases before coming to a stairway that rose in a seemingly endless curve.

"I shall wait here and guard our escape route," Elvira said. "For it is a very long way to the top."

"No need for both of us to wear ourselves out," Dan agreed and started climbing.

Laboring hard and breathing heavily and feeling as though he had climbed halfway to the clouds, he finally came upon a solitary door. He reversed his sword and pounded upon the portal with his hilt. "Meadows! Are you in there?"

"Bless you, Daniel!" The old man sounded close to tears. "Can that truly be you?"

"None other." Dan looked frantically about. "I don't see a key, though. How are we going to get you out? That door must be a foot thick."

"If I might be so bold," Napoleon said, prodding Dan with one forepaw. "I observe that there also appears to be no keyhole."

Dan wheeled back around, resisted the urge to scratch his head, and let his jaw fall to half-mast. "Oh."

"A simple lack of a handle on the inside," Napoleon observed, "would keep him trapped and still allow the count to declare that he has locked no one in."

"Who is that spouting wisdom to you, lad?" Meadows demanded.

"I do so hope you heard that," Napoleon said.

Dan turned the handle, pushed open the door, and said, "Let's get going while the going's good."

Meadows stepped out, grasped Dan by the shoulders, then looked about. "With whom were you speaking? I distinctly heard two voices."

"Indeed," Napoleon agreed. "One of them spouting wisdom, as you so rightly said."

Dan indicated the bunny in his pocket. "You remember Napoleon."

"So nice to see you again," Napoleon purred. "You are keeping well?"

"You?" Meadows collected himself and announced, "I have a surprise for you, lad."

"Unless it's three pairs of wings or an inflatable escape hatch," Dan said, "it needs to wait."

"Come and see," Meadows said, stepping back and motioning Dan toward a bundle stashed in the corner of his chamber.

"My weapons!"

"I knew you would come," Meadows proclaimed. "I *knew* it. I begged them to let me keep your things as a memento of my departed retainer. They thought themselves catering to an old man's harmless whims."

The sword fit his hand like an old friend. "This is great, Meadows. Just great."

Meadows beamed. "It was the least I could do for the rescuer I knew would come."

Napoleon sniffed noisily. "Smoke," he announced. "I distinctly smell smoke."

Dan strung the bow, then handed both it and the quivers to Meadows. "Can you carry them?"

"This and more. My limbs have been given new strength."

They clattered back down the stairs. When they arrived at the landing, the smoke was swirling thick. Elvira appeared before them like a great warrior woman. "It is glorious to see you again, Meadows."

"Elvira!" Meadows rushed over to embrace as much of her as he could manage. "Thank heavens you're all right!"

The stairway leading downward resounded with the shouts and cries and clamor of full-blown panic.

"Down is definitely out," Dan said. "Which way?"

"That is hard to say," Elvira replied worriedly. "Noise comes from every direction."

"Splendid, just splendid." Napoleon wriggled worriedly in Dan's pocket. "So why don't we just sit here and have a nice chitchat until they come looking for us?"

"I suppose you have heard the mouth on this little one," Elvira said to Meadows.

"We met several days ago," Meadows agreed.

"We'll just have to hope the smoke and confusion mask us," Dan decided. "Which is the fastest way to the front gates?"

This time the cook did not hesitate. She pointed down one side passage. "There."

"All right, then," Dan said. "Let's go!"

–Fifteen–

"You say there's no change in the patient's situation?" Dr. Glacey, the newly appointed resident psychiatrist, asked eagerly. He stood beside Dr. Prain in the hospital dressing chambers, pumping him as the doctor prepared for duty.

"The sleep-wakefulness schedule is still irregular," Dr. Prain replied stiffly. "But the overall pattern remains constant."

"And there is no medical reason for his state?"

"None that I have been able to find." Dr. Prain was finding it increasingly difficult to maintain control when discussing the Simmons patient.

Other doctors now associated him with the patient who wouldn't stay awake, and nothing else. His orderly ward, his meticulous records, his detailed and punctual reports, all were shoved aside unnoticed. Whenever he was met in the halls, in the dining room, or at staff conferences, the questions were always the same. It had even reached the point that he was being approached at social occasions and in public places by doctors he did not know. They all asked the same questions. It had become so predictable that whenever someone walked his way these days, his immediate response was "No change."

He was beginning to detest the Simmons patient and everything he stood for with a burning passion.

"And the girl?" the psychiatrist demanded.

"Her situation appears to be improving," Dr. Prain replied, neglecting to mention the fact that he had had nothing to do with the gradual change. He could neither explain why she had slept or why she was not waking up more regularly. He looked up from his locker and was immensely irritated to find that the entire changing room was now listening intently.

"She is spending an increasing amount of time awake, but still sleeps far more than normal," Prain went on, his voice even more clipped than usual. "Due to her adverse home environment, it was decided to keep her here under observation for another few days."

That had been Dr. Meadows' decision, much to his own helpless fury. Dr. Prain would have liked nothing more than to see the last of that irritating little child. But Dr. Meadows had used his seniority first to check with the social worker on the child's home life and then to order him, *order* him, to keep the child on.

The psychiatrist mulled over the information, as though making mental notes. "Have you had an opportunity to question them?"

"Several times." Dr. Prain stifled an oath as he tried to slide his arm into the sleeve of his hospital coat, only to have it stopped cold. The sleeve felt as rigid as a thin sheet of reinforced concrete. He liked the sharp-edged image of a well-starched coat, liked to finish his duty looking as fresh and well pressed as when he went on. He had asked the laundry staff to put a little extra starch in his coats, but this was absurd.

"There have been no indications of physical pain or discomfort?" Dr. Glacey pressed.

"None." Dr. Prain flapped the coat out in front of him, the stiff garment cracking like a whip. He jammed a fist down the sleeve, finally managing to insert one arm. But the other simply would not budge. What had the idiots done, starched his coat with super glue? He took it off, flapped it again. For some reason, he found himself blaming the Simmons kid for this. No question about it. He was really beginning to *hate* that kid.

Dr. Glacey asked, "Have you checked for possible psychological trauma?"

Dr. Prain lifted his attention from the coat. This was something new. "What?"

"From his accident. That's what brought him in here, wasn't it?"

"That's right. A car accident."

Dr. Glacey leaned forward. He was an intense man whose dark close-cropped curls held his sharp-featured face in a wiry grip. His name was already being established in the circles Dr. Prain wished he could enter.

Dr. Prain had tried to read one of the man's articles; he liked to keep his finger on what everyone else was doing. In the article he had read, Dr. Glacey's first sentence was seventeen lines long. By the third paragraph Dr. Prain had felt as though he were lunching on sleeping pills.

"I've been making a study of post-accident trauma," Dr. Glacey announced excitedly.

"Great," Dr. Prain mumbled, utterly at a loss.

"It's an entirely new field. It occurs to me that your patient might be refusing to wake up because subconsciously he wishes to avoid accepting the shock and fear-factor resulting from his accident."

"What you're suggesting," Dr. Prain said, "is that my patient has scared himself to sleep?"

"In effect," Dr. Glacey replied.

"I see." Dr. Prain finally succeeded in jamming his second arm down the sleeve and began the laborious process of trying to force the buttons through starch-sealed holes. It gave him something to do, instead of telling the psychiatrist that his theory sounded to him like something straight from Looney Tunes.

"I'd like to speak with him, if you don't mind."

"Be my guest," Dr. Prain said.

"When do you expect him to wake up again?"

Dr. Prain jammed his name tag through the slick-hard surface of his coat, then checked in the mirror to see that the tag was exactly level and his hair was neat. "For the past several days he has made an appearance every fourteen to eighteen hours."

"An appearance," Dr. Glacey said, making another of his mental notes. "That's good. I must remember that."

"He should be coming around sometime this morning," Dr. Prain went on, making a final adjustment to the knot of his tie. He kept his opinions to himself as he turned back to the overly intense psychiatrist. Why not let the man go play with his theories? Spread the blame around as far as possible. "Check with Elvira, the head ward nurse. She'll contact you when the monitor goes off."

Dan opened his eyes to find Consuela seated beside his hospital bed.

"This is very strange," she announced.

"You made it back," Dan said. His head felt heavy. "Good."

"I don't see what's so great about it," she said, a little

frown creasing her brow. "How do I get back?"

"All I know is that when I fall asleep again, I'm there. So far, anyway." Dan found it difficult to raise his arm. "Could you give me some water?"

She picked up the glass, fitted in the straw, and said, "What happened to you?"

He drank deep, sighed, laid his head back flat. For some reason he felt exhausted by the effort. "You mean why am I here in the hospital?"

"Yes."

"Accident. Got sideswiped by a truck. I was making a delivery in a snowstorm."

She put her little hands on her hips and said fiercely, "What were you doing driving in that kind of weather?"

He smiled. "I had a part-time job for the holidays, and I needed the money." He examined her head. "They told me you got knocked out when you hit a table. You look okay."

"I feel fine," she said, touching a small bruise on her forehead. "All I know is, I was in the kitchen talking to the social worker, and then I woke up with all these doctors standing around my bed."

Social worker. Dan surveyed her dark hair and eyes, asked, "Where is your family from?"

"Here. My dad's Hispanic, but my mom's Anglo," she said in a matter-of-fact manner that was much more mature than her nine years would suggest. "I don't remember my dad so good. He left when I was little."

"I'm sorry," Dan said. He hesitated, then added, "My parents are both dead. My dad was an amateur pilot, and they crashed in a storm a couple of years ago."

Her dark eyes filled with genuine sorrow. "That must have been hard."

He nodded, and wondered again why every little effort

was such a strain. "It was. I've lived buried in school and work since then."

"Do you have any brothers and sisters?"

"One sister. She sort of went on a permanent vacation when it happened. She comes back to earn money, then takes off again. What about you?"

Consuela shook her head. In that same matter-of-fact tone she said, "Just me and my mom. She's an alcoholic."

"Hey, that's tough."

She shrugged dismissively. "That's okay."

Dan gave her a frank inspection. She was a truly beautiful child, in a dark pixielike way. Her hair was long and so jet black it shined like a polished mirror. Her eyes were like opals, clear and sparkling with intelligent awareness. "Yeah, it looks like you're gonna be okay, regardless."

Her gaze was equally frank. "I was pretty nasty to you over there, wasn't I?"

"Forget it." Dan grinned. "If somebody showed up in one of my own daydreams and I couldn't get rid of him, I'd be pretty hot myself."

She did not return his smile. "It's real, though, isn't it?"

Dan sobered. "I don't know what's going on, and I can't explain it. But yeah, I think it's as real as anything in this crazy world."

"I think so too." She inspected him for a moment longer, then said, "I've got some bad news. I hate to give it to you when you're not well, though."

"I'm okay, just a little weak," Dan replied. "What's the matter?"

"They stole the Book," she said sadly.

"I know," Dan replied. "There's one in the drawer there."

"What?"

"Your room has one too."

"What are you talking about?"

"Open the drawer and see."

Half expecting to find he was making fun of her, she pulled the drawer out and gave a little gasp. Hesitantly she pulled out the Book, opened the cover, and said, "It *is* real."

"I told you," Dan said. "Read me something." Then he remembered her age. "No, that's okay. I can—"

She understood him perfectly. "I can read good," she said hotly. "It's all I've ever had to do, that and go there."

Dan nodded, for some reason understanding her better than he'd ever understood anyone. And in accepting this, he found himself so full of compassion for the young girl that he felt his heart swelling up too large for his chest. "I'm sure you read better than I do," he said softly. "Read me something. Please."

She bent back over the open page. Then she half spoke, half whispered, "I'm really sorry about what I said to you."

He made a vast effort, and managed to raise his arm and settle his hand upon hers. "It's okay. Really. Pals?"

She lifted her head, her eyes bright, and nodded.

"It's amazing how you look at the Book and somehow see yourself better, isn't it?" Dan said.

"I like it," she agreed. "But it's *hard*."

"You're a good kid," he said.

For some reason that brought her almost to tears. She gathered herself and said, "There's something more I need to tell you."

Dan thought immediately of Cousteau and could not bear to hear about the old man. "Not yet," he said. "I need to take the bad news in small doses." Then he remembered. "Listen, you know the nurse here called Elvira?"

"Sure. She's nice."

"She's more than that," Dan said. "She should be showing up sometime today. I mean, tomorrow. Or whatever it is."

Consuela cocked her head to one side. "You mean, over there?"

"Yes. She'll be with Meadows."

Her eyes grew wider by degrees. "Like the Dr. Meadows here?"

"Crazy, isn't it?"

"Dr. Meadows and Elvira are both over there?" When she got surprised like this, her voice rose to the pitch of an excited little girl.

"Or both of them are over here," Dan said. It was amazing, Dan thought, to be with someone who was both so mature and so young at the same time. "I personally can't make heads or tails of the whole thing."

She looked at him with wonder-filled eyes. "This is incredible."

"You're telling me." He refrained from saying anything about Cousteau. He did not want to hear that news. Not yet. "So is that other doctor."

"Prain. Yech." She made a face. "I don't like him. He's always walking around with his little clipboard. He makes me feel like I'm part of a paper factory, like I'm here for him to make out the forms."

"I know just what you mean," Dan said. "But it's worse than that. At least over there. He's so caught up in being correct and in control, he's gone off the deep end." He smiled. "But I got him."

"How?"

Briefly Dan told her about the castle and the fire. "Meadows and Elvira are coming back with the horse. They'll put some supplies together and send the horse back to us. Napoleon said he wanted to come with me. We're off to find the Tower of Abandon, whatever that is."

"Cousteau doesn't like to talk about it," Consuela said.

Dan took a breath. "Okay, you might as well give it to me."

Her face turned sadder than her young years should allow. "It's about—"

The door pushed open to reveal a young doctor with dark curly hair cropped close to his head. "You're awake! Excellent, excellent." He frowned at Consuela. "What are you doing in here, young lady?"

Something about the man's attitude irritated Dan immensely. "She's in here because I want her in here," he replied sharply. "Which is more than I can say for you."

The man did a mental retreat and put on an air of totally false friendliness. "Hey, there's no need for that. I'm just here to help."

"I better go," Consuela said, closing the Book and rising from her chair.

"What's that you've got there, young lady?" The doctor moved up close enough to see what Consuela held.

"Nothing," Consuela said, replacing the Book in the drawer. To Dan she said, "I'll come back later and read to you."

"I may not be here," Dan said, ignoring the doctor's expression as he looked from the closed drawer to Consuela and back again.

"I'll wait," Consuela promised.

"No, that is," the doctor cleared his throat. "I'm not sure it's a good idea—"

"That'd be great," Dan said to Consuela and felt the familiar tide of fatigue rising up to engulf him.

Consuela reached over to touch his shoulder. "I have to tell you something."

"I know," Dan said sleepily. "Cousteau."

"No," she said, surprised. "He's fine. It's Bliss. She's gone. They took her."

Dan struggled to fight off the fatigue and rise back and ask for details, but despite his own desire and the young doctor's cry of frustration, he could not. His eyelids closed, and he was away.

–Sixteen–

Dan's passage was again lit by the sun that was more than a sun, a light that was both distant and yet shone within his own heart. He passed the waterfall and found himself slowing, descending, gradually settling in a brilliant green clearing where Cousteau stood waiting for him.

Before he could ask about Bliss, the old man stated solemnly, "I am here as a messenger. You must take heed, Knight Daniel, for ahead of you lies a crossroads."

The words were carried to Dan upon a force so great that they blew straight through him, stripping away all ability to think of anything other than what the old man said.

Old, yet no longer old. For the man stood cloaked in a wisdom so powerful that he transcended age. "You have been granted two great gifts, young knight. But for the second to flourish, you must relinquish the first." Cousteau gestured. "Come closer."

Dan found himself swept up by the same power that had given Cousteau's voice the power of a whirlwind. He did not step forward. He was *placed* there.

He stood beside Cousteau and looked down, and realized he was gazing upon the Book.

"In the early pages," Cousteau said, "man is taught as one who lives and dies by the sword. As one who requires ritual to give form and definition to his life. As one who lives by the force of deed. By might of arms and valor in battle."

He lifted up a section of pages and pushed them over. Again, and a third time, working his way further and further into the Book. As he did so, the light grew ever stronger.

A fourth turning, and the light was so powerful it illuminated everything it touched from within and without, carrying the same power as the sun that was more than a sun.

"Here begins the Book's second and final section," Cousteau announced. "And for you to proceed upon the Way charted upon these pages, you must lay down your weapons. You must relinquish your power with the sword. You must give up hate and anger and desire for revenge. You must look *beyond*. You must grow past who you are, to become who you are invited to be."

Cousteau's voice was soft and grave, yet its authority was so great the words reverberated through Dan like lightning bolts crashing down around him.

"Become a knight of love, Daniel. The invitation stands before you. Gird yourself with righteousness. Take up the shield of faith and the sword of the Spirit, and carry them upon feet strengthened by the gospel of peace. And thus, Knight Daniel, shall you become one of the force *eternal*."

The final word was too powerful. It shot him away like a leaf blasted by a hurricane. He was flung so far and so fast that everything about him melted into a grayish blur of speed and power within which the word continued to resound.

Eternal.

— SEVENTEEN —

Dan awoke to find Napoleon fast asleep on his chest.

The little bunny was emitting soft snores no louder than a kitten's purr. Dan craned downward, but all he could see were a fluffy white tail and two chocolate-brown hind legs sprawled out flat. The bunny's cool nose was nestled in the soft point of his throat.

Dan lay there for a while, smiling as the bunny snuggled up closer under his chin. When the sun looked ready to rise above the trees surrounding their meadow, he shut his eyes once more, grunted, shook himself, and pretended to come awake. He rolled over, opened his eyes, and said, "Good morning."

By then Napoleon was seated on his haunches beside Dan, calmly washing his face. "Finally decided to join us, did you? How nice."

Dan sat up, stretched, and asked, "Been up long?"

"Hours." Napoleon pointed over toward the trees. "Your horse is back."

And so it was. Dan whistled, and the steed came trotting over. Around its neck was a halter, and tied to the halter were a sack of provisions and two drinking skins.

At the top of the sack was a note from Cousteau. Dan unrolled the stiff parchment and read,

> *Your valiant steed arrived safely, bearing Meadows and Elvira. They have done much to make your bravery live for us. The news they brought has raised our spirits in a bleak time.*
>
> *I regret to report that Bliss was taken in the night. By whom and where I cannot say for certain, but I fear it was to the place I do not care to name. I cannot advise you to seek her there, yet must accept that it is perhaps part of your quest. If so, I can but offer the advice of one who has only observed from afar: There lies a world ruled by fear and hopelessness. It will seek to ignite desires which are self-consuming and self-destructive. Whatever gifts it offers will only drive these killing desires deeper into your being. Its speech is based upon lies. What it promises it does not deliver. The closer you come, the more tightly will the cloak of darkness draw around your heart.*
>
> *You must therefore see with the Light which pierces all shadows, and walk with the strength of wisdom found in truth and in love.*
>
> *Your friend,*
> *Cousteau*

Dan looked up to find Napoleon watching him. He said, "Bliss has been taken."

The rabbit teetered but forced itself to remain upright. "Where?"

"Cousteau didn't say for sure, but it sounds like she's in the Tower of Abandon, whatever that is."

"You don't seem all that shocked and distressed," Napoleon observed.

"I already knew. Consuela told me last night . . ." He

hesitated, then finished, ". . . in a dream."

"How convenient," the bunny said. "Do you two chat often?"

"This was the first time."

"I don't suppose you asked her to pack anything for me. A little alfalfa, perhaps?"

"The horse was already gone." He rummaged in the sack. "But if I know Cousteau, he wouldn't forget his favorite talking bunny."

Napoleon's little nose lifted into the air and twitched nervously. "Is that what I think I smell?"

"I wouldn't know," Dan replied, digging deeper. "But I remember that the bunny my sister had used to love—"

"Strawberries," the rabbit said and began to hop in place.

Dan looked over and grinned. "Yeah, my sister's rabbit used to do the bunny two-step for strawberries too."

"Don't tease. Please, please, please let me have a strawberry *now*."

Dan lifted out a small sack, opened the top, pulled out a beautiful ripe strawberry, and set it down on the grass. "Enjoy."

"Mmmmmm." Napoleon literally dived onto the plump red fruit. His sharp little teeth made an ever deeper incision as he ate. Dan watched and munched on a piece of bread.

When the strawberry was reduced to a gnawed little cap like a bit of wet green felt, Napoleon sat back on his haunches and announced, "That was absolutely divine."

"More?" Dan set another berry down beside the rabbit.

"Thank you. They must have come up just since we left. The first strawberries of the season." His little nose was all pink with strawberry goo. "I dream about them in wintertime, you know. I really do." He bent over and munched contentedly, then raised himself and asked, "What do you dream about, when you're not having conversations with sharp-tongued little girls?"

"Hard to say." Dan took a long pull from the leather drinking skin. "Mostly about home."

"Do you miss it?" Napoleon nodded his thanks as Dan set a third strawberry down before him. He touched it with a forepaw, savoring the pleasure to come.

"Sometimes. Not too often." His feelings about home were all jumbled up, so he pushed them away and said, "It's still winter where I'm from. We just had a really bad snowstorm."

Napoleon regarded him gravely. "It must be very far away to have different seasons."

"It is," Dan agreed quietly, his thoughts elsewhere.

"You were not thinking about home then, though." The bunny observed him with chocolate-colored eyes. "You miss her a lot, don't you?"

Dan nodded. "Bliss is the best thing that's ever happened to me."

"She's the best thing that's happened to a lot of us," Napoleon replied.

"So where do you think she is?"

"No question. She's been taken to the Tower of Abandon. Nothing else makes sense." Napoleon rolled the third strawberry toward Dan. "Pack that up for later, will you? Suddenly I've lost my appetite."

Dan put the strawberry back into the sack and twisted the top closed. "Can you tell me anything about it?"

The bunny shrugged its minuscule shoulders. "Not much. The Tower of Abandon is set upon the mountains that ring the world of man."

"Yeah? What's beyond those mountains?"

"Fairies and dragons and windswept seas, of course.

What else?" The bunny cocked his head to one side. "You are the great traveler. Why on earth are you asking me that?"

"No reason. Go ahead."

"That's all I know."

Dan rose to his feet. "I guess we'd better be making tracks, then." He lifted his little friend and settled Napoleon in his vest pocket. "You have any idea which way we need to go?"

"Ride away from the light," Napoleon replied. "That's all I ever heard. When the talk got to that point, I always scampered for the nearest hole."

"That sounds clear enough, I guess," Dan said, grasping the horse's mane and swinging himself onto its back. "Come on. Let's get this show on the road."

They arrived back at the same meadow late that afternoon. Again.

"By my count," Napoleon announced, "this makes our thirty-seventh visit."

"I'm well and truly stumped," Dan replied, scouting the surrounding forest. "We have now tried every single track and furrow leading out of here."

"Twice," Napoleon agreed.

"And every one of them has taken us in a giant circle." He looked down at his little friend. "Any ideas?"

"Home might be nice," Napoleon suggested.

The horse snorted its endorsement of the suggestion.

Dan looked out over the vista of green pastures and said, "Has either of you gotten the idea that somebody doesn't want us to go where we're headed?"

"Home," Napoleon repeated. "It's looking better to me all the time."

"Not with Bliss trapped somewhere out there," Dan replied, sliding from the horse's back. He lifted Napoleon from his pocket and settled the bunny on the horse's back.

"What are you doing?" Napoleon demanded.

"I want to try something," Dan replied. He walked around to stand in front of the horse. "I'm going to close my eyes and walk for a while. Just follow behind me, okay? Even if it doesn't look like there's a path or anything."

"That doesn't make one iota of sense to me," Napoleon declared. He nudged the horse's neck. "Does it make any sense to you?"

The horse snorted loudly and shook its head from side to side.

"If it looks like I'm going off a cliff or something," Dan persisted, "grab the back of my shirt but let me keep going."

"Crazy and crazier," Napoleon announced. "What happens if you sprout wings and start to fly away?"

"Okay," Dan said, turning around. "Quiet in the peanut gallery." He shut his eyes. Part of him agreed that it was crazy. Another part, however, told him it was the only chance he had left.

He tried to stop hearing the birds chirping, to ignore the wind's gentle pressure on his skin, to disregard the horse's breathing and Napoleon's quiet muttering, and concentrate. Concentrate. Concentrate.

The sliver of metal around his neck seemed to vibrate. Not against his skin, but in time to the cadence of his heart. Reaching out, pointing forward, searching for the point where Bliss was waiting.

There.

Dan kept his eyes closed and started walking forward.

"I suppose I should mention," Napoleon announced, "that you are now walking toward the thickest thornbush I have ever seen in my life."

"Quiet," Dan said, his voice soft but sharp. "I have to concentrate."

He kept walking, his newfound vision certain as his heartbeat. The noisy part of his own mind kept waiting for the thorns to snag and to tear. But his newfound heart's voice continued to reach out, certain of the direction.

His path remained clear.

"Ahem," Napoleon said. "I believe a bunny's apologies are in order."

"Shhh," Dan said and kept walking.

They continued in silent progression for a while. The only time Dan faltered was when he began listening to the doubting chatter in his mind. Then he would stop, take several deep breaths, and return his concentration to the compass in his heart. Then he walked on.

After a long time of silent walking, Napoleon quietly announced, "We have arrived."

Dan opened his eyes and saw that indeed they had.

The tower was surrounded not by a moat, but rather by a lake so large it could only be called an inland sea. The water was steel gray and untouched by the evening breeze, and threatened to hold hidden terrors in its unseen depths.

Mountains ringed the sea, and dark clouds loomed above the peaks. Gray waters extended to the mountains, and the mountains to great rumbling thunderheads. The tower was surrounded by barriers that reached from earth to the highest heavens. Dan stood at the water's edge, feeling smaller than he ever had in his entire life, and knew that daylight would never reach here. This was a place held in perpetual dusk.

The rock he stood upon would never permit life. It had the dark sheen of frozen lava, hard and unyielding and utterly dead. The entire shoreline was formed from this sullen stone.

Dan lifted his gaze and looked upon the tower itself. It rose from its great stone island like some inhuman growth, tall and dark and as blank faced as the rock upon which it stood. The lower levels were almost as craggy as the island, but slowly it smoothed out, becoming an octagon, then a hexagon, then a square. Higher still, up at a level just below the encircling clouds, the angles smoothed out entirely and the tower became a dark and brooding cone. At its very peak there burned a crimson flame.

With enormous effort Dan turned his back to the tower, and in doing so broke free from its hopeless hold. "Come on," he said, his words swallowed by the emptiness that surrounded them. "Let's have a bite to eat and get some rest."

For once Napoleon had nothing to say.

– Eighteen –

Dan was being pushed down a long gray-green hall by a very big hospital orderly. The wheelchair had one wheel that needed oil. It gave a little peeping sound with each revolution. The sound was all that Dan could use to keep himself focused on the here and now.

He had awaked to an empty chamber, but it seemed that hardly seconds had passed before the door had flown open to emit Elvira, an orderly, and the snippy dark-haired doctor. The doctor had popped off orders, which Dan was still too bleary to understand, then spun about and departed.

The orderly had flipped back the covers and lifted Dan as easily as he would a little child. He had said something about the psychiatrist wanting to see Dan in his own office. In his very pleasant voice, the orderly had then said something about the beautiful winter day as they passed a window. Dan had wanted to respond but could not.

Dan remained encapsulated within an invisible shield. Inside these confines of his inert body, he felt strangely alive. Alert. As though coming fully awake for the first time in his life. The outside world was filtered, but at the same time what broke through he heard with absolute clarity.

High above his hearing range cried a high-pitched keening. It was softer than the hiss of air through the overhead vent, but more easily heard than the loudspeaker, the orderly, the clump and clatter of a hospital hallway.

And he did not hear it with his ears.

It was as though the sense he had awakened by following the unseen path would not now be stilled. Dan allowed himself to be rolled down the bustling hallway and heard more clearly than anything in his life the soft cry of another heart in need.

His heart was hearing a voice of fear, he knew. It called to him, not to anyone else. It pleaded. It spoke without words in desperate craving for help.

"What's going on here?" Dr. Prain stepped out from the nurses' station and blocked the orderly's way.

"Dr. Glacey told me to bring the patient to his office," the orderly replied. "Something about trying to keep him awake by changing his surroundings. I thought he had already spoken with you."

"Oh, yes. Right." For some reason, Dr. Prain was momentarily flustered by the news. Dan kept his head lowered, not wanting to even see the man. "Just a minute, let me make a call."

When the orderly stepped into the station behind the doctor, Dan lifted his head and searched for the source of the sound. It came from a nearby room, that much he was sure of. He looked from door to door until the internal awakening in his heart signaled that this was the one. The feeling was like the chiming of a fine crystal goblet, soft yet unmistakable.

Dan forced his arms to grasp the wheels of his chair and roll him over to the door. He knocked softly, then made the effort to raise one hand and turn the knob. As the door opened, he asked, "Is everything all right?"

"What? Who—"

Dan pushed the door open farther and rolled his chair into view. "My name is Dan. I'm a patient here too. Is everything all right?"

An old woman picked at her coverlet. Her hand had the nervous movement of a frail little bird. She worked her mouth for a moment, then whispered, "The doctors say I have to have another operation."

Dan rolled his chair over to the side of her bed. The effort exhausted him. He set his hands on her mattress as much for support as to be close to her. "And you don't want to?"

"I've had so many," the old woman replied. "I don't feel as though I have any strength left."

Dan nodded. That he could understand.

A tear escaped and trickled down her ravaged cheek. "If they put me to sleep, I don't think I'm going to wake up again."

Something in the clarity of his heart said this was true.

Her toothless mouth worked for a moment, then she whispered shakily. "I'm afraid of dying all alone."

The crystal bell of his heart tolled out words that were offered up for him to say. And with them came a gift of light. Of love. Of peace.

"You're not alone," Dan said softly. "You're never alone."

He gripped her hand with both of his and willed her to accept the gift of so much love and comfort he knew he would never be able to hold it all within his own heart. "There is One who is always by your side. Even when your time comes, you will find Him standing by the doorway, ready to help you enter."

The old woman stared at him with rheumy eyes. Her hand gripped his with desperate strength. "Would you pray with me?" she whispered.

Dan nodded, bowed his head, and spoke the words that rose like a tide of crystal bubbles, lifting up through the great sea of love and swelling his heart to a new fullness. "O Father in heaven, you alone know the mysteries of life."

Dan spoke the words and yet hardly heard them, knowing that in truth they were not meant for him at all. When he was finished he raised his head, met her gaze with his, and shared with her the gift of peace.

"Hey!" The orderly appeared in the doorway and said with barely controlled panic, "What are you doing in here, man? Trying to get us both in trouble?"

Dan gave the lady's hand a final squeeze. "You are not alone," he repeated.

"Well, now," the wiry-haired doctor said, waving the orderly away. "How are we feeling today?"

"Weak," Dan said, taking a look around. The office was in a high corner of the hospital. Its dual windows overlooked the parking lot, a busy street, and a forest beyond. But Dan's eye was caught by the great expanse of sky, with scuttling clouds and vast swatches of blue and sunlight. He drank in the sight, storing it away for his return to the land of gloom and gray.

"That is certainly understandable," Dr. Glacey replied, "considering how much you have been sleeping. But a few sessions with a good physical therapist should see you right." He steepled his hands on the desk before him and said, "Tell me, Dan—may I call you Dan?"

"Sure."

"Tell me, do you remember anything about your accident?"

"Of course."

The doctor faltered and then caught himself. "Why 'of course'?"

Dan gave him a sideways look. "I was there, wasn't I?"

"Yes, but what can you tell me about it?"

The doctor's fakey friendliness was beginning to wear thin. "I was driving to work in a snowstorm," Dan said impatiently. "A truck ran a stoplight. I guess he couldn't stop on the ice. He slammed into me, lifted my van up, and turned it over. The next thing I knew, I woke up in the hospital."

The doctor doodled on his pad, clearly disappointed by something Dan had said. "How did it feel?"

Who was this guy? "Like getting hit by a ton of bricks," Dan said impatiently. "Look, can you do something for me?"

"What's that, Dan?"

"Can you get me assigned to a different doctor?"

He showed a keener interest. "Why, Dan? What's the matter with Dr. Prain?"

"Let's just say he rubs me the wrong way."

"Dr. Prain happens to be a highly qualified doctor, Dan. He's done everything possible to make you better."

"The best way he could help me," Dan replied, "is to leave me alone."

Dr. Glacey eyed him thoughtfully for a moment. "I suppose I could help you, Dan. That is, if you were to decide to fully cooperate."

"Cooperate with what?" Dan asked.

Dr. Glacey leaned across his desk. "Why are you sleeping so much, Dan? Do you feel you're trying to avoid something?"

"Like what?"

"Anything. The accident, for instance. Does it make you uncomfortable to think about it?"

"I hardly think about it at all," Dan replied truthfully.

That pleased the doctor enormously. He made a little notation, then asked, "Do you find sleep welcoming, Dan? Are your dreams more pleasant than being awake?"

Dan thought of Bliss, gave a faint smile and replied, "Sometimes."

"And other times?"

"You don't want to know."

"Oh, but I do, Dan. I really do."

Dan eyed the doctor. "And if I tell you this, you'll have me assigned to another doctor?"

"I will certainly try and help you any way I can, Dan." The doctor forced himself to play at a casual attitude. "So tell me about these dreams of yours."

"They're not really dreams," Dan replied. He took a breath, and told him.

"This is a textbook case of post-accident trauma," Dr. Glacey announced excitedly. "I have never heard of a more vividly clear example."

Dr. Prain was less than eager to hear the news. "So you've cured him, have you?"

"Well, no. These things take time, of course. But at least we have gotten to the root of his ailment."

Not we, you, Dr. Prain corrected silently. And when it came time for the psychiatrist to write up his findings for the journals, the only mention Dr. Prain would receive would be as the doctor who had struggled for weeks to cure the patient and gotten nowhere. "How can you be so sure?"

"Listen, he thinks that when he's asleep he's transported to a different world." Dr. Glacey was almost dancing in place, he was so excited. "His desire to avoid facing up to the shock of his accident has empowered this dreamworld with amazingly vivid details."

"So he has intense dreams," Dr. Prain said grumpily. "So what?"

"That's not all," Dr. Glacey replied, clearly saving the best for last. "He asked me to have him assigned to another doctor."

"What!"

Dr. Glacey nodded vigorously. "Clearly he realizes that you have been striving to wake him up. He has therefore assigned you a negative role in this dreamworld of his."

Dr. Prain felt his rage rising. The ungrateful little pest. "So what's the cure?"

Dr. Glacey assumed a professorial air. "There are two highly divergent opinions on that. One school takes the therapy route, suggesting that with time the patient would be willing to accept the truth and set his hallucinations aside. The other says it is best to apply a shock during the period of avoidance. Make it unpleasant for the patient to elude reality."

Dr. Prain recalled the loud whistle Dr. Meadows had given, and said, "That makes sense."

"Of course," Dr. Glacey added, "for a patient as deeply involved in his escape routine as this Simmons boy is, it would have to be a fairly massive shock. One repeated several times, I would imagine."

Dr. Prain had a brainstorm. He wheeled around and said over his shoulder, "You just leave that with me."

"Wait," Dr. Glacey protested.

"He's my patient," Dr. Prain called back as he hastened down the hall. "I'll decide what treatment is required!"

−Nineteen−

They ate a cheerless breakfast under a lowering sky.

The gray sea and mountains and sky were more than a gloomy color. They formed an oppressive force, one which held the companions down, sucked from them the will to resist or struggle or strive or succeed.

Dan packed up their remaining supplies and tied the sack to the horse's halter. He then placed the rabbit upon the steed's back and said, "If I'm not back by evening, leave without me. Don't spend another night in this place."

It was to Napoleon's credit that he did not give voice to his doubts or try to dissuade Dan from what looked to be a hopeless task. Instead he replied, "When you find Bliss, tell her we all want her to come home."

Home. The word held little meaning in this place. Dan nodded. "Will do."

"How," the rabbit began, then stopped and looked out over the lake. The water's surface was the color of slate and slick as a mirror, yet no reflection rose from its brooding surface. Beyond it, the High Tower loomed in ominous silence, crowned by the ever-burning crimson flame.

"Best not to ask," Dan agreed quietly. He reached out

one finger and caressed the little bunny. "You're a good friend, Napoleon."

"Go," the bunny said quietly. "Go now, so that you may return the sooner."

Dan stroked the soft furry pelt a moment longer, then patted the horse's flank, turned, and walked to the edge of the lake.

The inland sea greeted his arrival by immediately rearing up with waves five times his height.

There was no wind, no sudden rise of storm. Just the waves, looming and booming down upon the rocky shore like great hungry beasts.

Dan stood and watched and felt his weaker voice quail. Yet there was now within him a second voice, a new heart, one which left him with no doubt as to what he should do.

Slowly, deliberately, Dan set aside his weapons.

When the sword and bow and quiver and knives were all neatly laid upon the rock, he took a breath, closed his eyes, and waited.

It didn't work.

He opened his eyes once again. The quaking voice within his head had painted his closed eyelids with visions of beasts and demons and whirlwinds of destruction. The frenzy without was mirrored by the weaker voice within. Dan stood and looked out over the furiously pounding surf and knew there was an answer, yet found it not.

And then it came.

In the midst of hopeless ruin there shone a Light which was unseen by his physical eyes. Dan could not explain it, did not know how he could be so sure of something felt and not seen. Yet he was. The Light was so clear and so powerful, and answered so unconditionally by the chiming within his heart, that Dan had no choice.

He stepped into the raging waters.

And the waters solidified and held him aloft.

The waves became the beasts of his darkened mind, taking the form of fanged demons who stormed and raged and demanded that he fear them. Dan held desperately to his nerve and kept his eyes focused straight ahead, upon the Light which shone for his heart and not for his physical eyes.

Dr. Prain raced along the hall, fairly flew down the stairs, and spotted a gray-uniformed janitor mopping the ground floor. He grasped the man by his arm and demanded, "Do you have the keys to the cellars?"

"I might," the man answered. "If you let go of my arm."

Dr. Prain dropped his hand. "Come with me," he snapped.

The hospital cellars were voluminous, lined with roughly painted concrete blocks and containing a series of gray steel doors. It had been one of Dr. Prain's thankless tasks as a new resident to catalogue some of the junk that had already accumulated there. He led the janitor past the rooms containing the laundry and stores to a final trio of doors stenciled with letters and numbers.

He pointed to the middle door and snapped, "Open this one."

The janitor did so, then stepped back when the doctor flung the door open, flicked on the light, and walked inside.

The same month that the hospital had opened, the old community mental institute had been closed. The patients were relocated to a separate building of the new hospital compound. Many of the old instruments had found their way down into this cellar.

Dr. Prain stumbled through the dusty clutter and

shouted back at the janitor, "Help me clear this stuff out of the way."

"What for?"

"Just do it!" Dr. Prain made it to the back of the room. There it was, just as he had remembered it. He flipped back the heavy dust cover and stared down at the enormous machine. If only it still worked.

The janitor moved up beside him and stared with bulging eyes at the machine. "What in the world is that?"

"An electroshock therapy machine," Dr. Prain replied with enormous satisfaction.

The janitor hefted what appeared to be a pair of oversized headphones, except where the earpieces should have been, there were a pair of very solid, heavy balls. "You stick this thing on somebody's head?"

"Right on the temples," Dr. Prain agreed. "Then you adjust the level of electrical charge with that dial and flip this lever."

The janitor shook his head. "I've seen some weird stuff in my days," he said, "but this takes the cake."

Dr. Prain knelt and looked underneath. "It has wheels. We should be able to roll it."

"Like a torture instrument from the laboratory of a mad scientist," the janitor muttered. "Who comes up with this stuff?"

"Okay now," Dr. Prain said, squeezing in behind the machine. "Push!"

The distance was crossed, the shore made. Dan clambered up the rise of burn-blackened rock. As soon as his head rose above the precipice, a chorus of wolves was there to greet him.

They howled like banshees in a storm-filled night. Their

eyes were red as coals in a smoldering fire. Their tongues lolled, their fangs drooled, and about their necks rose great manes of silver-black hair.

Dan stood and heard the still small voice call to him, and knew that he must force aside his fear. Yet it was hard, so hard to heed the unspoken call and not the howling wolves. And in that moment's hesitation he lost the direction of the voice and moved instead toward a door that appeared to offer the only safety from the wolves. He pushed it open.

"Welcome," a voice said, drawing him into the chamber. "I am your host. What can I get you?"

"Nothing," Dan said. He couldn't focus upon the speaker, as he remained in a perpetual half-shadow.

"Nonsense," his host replied. "You must be tired after your hard journey. Would you care to rest?"

"Not here," Dan said. "All I want is to get what I came for and leave." And yet the offer of rest was so inviting. He *was* tired. And here was such a comfortable chair. Suddenly Dan felt as though his legs were barely able to keep him upright.

"You mustn't believe that feeble old man's foolish tales," the host soothed. "Cousteau is just out to trick you, you know. He doesn't care anything about you, except as one more person he might enslave. Just as he is himself the slave of that ridiculous old book. Do you know what's happened to him since we were all finally rid of that moldy old thing? Why, he has collapsed like a tent without its pegs."

"That's why I have to take the Book to him," Dan said, but his will was being sapped with his strength. He collapsed into the chair by the window and felt a keening sigh of defeat run through his heart.

The voice dripped honey like a soothing balm. "I hold the genuine power, you know. Look about you and see what is real. It is mine to give, to share with those I like. Whatever you want, just name it and it shall be yours. You wish to be a knight? Splendid. I am not one to demand the impossible from you. I would make you into everything you want and more. I hereby name you Chief Knight of all the lands. You see? Everything is in my power, and all that I have is yours."

Dan struggled to tamp down the excitement caused by the sudden rush of power that surged through him. He knew that it was not an idle offer. All he had to do was say yes, and the power of knighthood throughout all the land would be his.

And yet, all the while, the soft sigh of keening sadness whispered through his being, and gave him the strength to say, "For starters, I want the Book of Light."

"Whatever for? Of course, if that's what you want, you can have it. Didn't I say you could have anything you liked? But why should you ask for that absurd old book? Why not ask for power instead? *Real* power. Then you can go out and write your *own* book."

"And I want Bliss," Dan said, his determination quaking under the tempting spell.

"Bliss? Of course you can have her. But why bother with an empty-headed little thing who knows no better than to talk to animals, when instead you can have these?"

And with his last word, the host raised his hand, and from an unseen door sprang a trio of beauties dressed in diaphanous robes. They did not walk toward him, they *melted* into the folds of the chair, which somehow was rising up around him, encompassing him, encircling him. But Dan saw only the seductive charms of the three eager, willing beauties who draped themselves upon him.

Until he happened to glance through the window.

Outside, the fog was growing thicker. And thicker. And thicker still.

Despite his growing desire to stay and indulge and drink from the cup of power, Dan struggled to pull himself to his feet.

"I really think I should go look for myself," he said, his voice thick with choked-down longing.

"Of course you should," the host replied, instantly at his side. "Only, before you go, take one little look at this, would you?"

"No, I really do need to be going," Dan said, and suddenly for the life of him could not remember how long he had been there. Was it an hour? Or a year? Or a lifetime?

"Certainly you do," the host soothed, his voice immensely calming. He waved a dark, liquid hand at something Dan had for some reason failed to see before, perhaps because it was tucked away in the corner opposite the entrance. Or exit.

Dan found himself reluctant to shift his gaze from the door, as though watching it had suddenly become very important. But the host's gently shifting robe momentarily flowed before his eyes, and naturally Dan looked elsewhere, and gazed where he was directed.

"You see," the host said in his tranquilizing voice. "I wave my hand thus, and look what appears."

"A moving hologram," Dan said. "What is this, a virtual reality video game?"

"How apt a name," the host said. "Virtual reality."

"I heard they were coming out with them," Dan said. "I've never seen one before."

"Well, now is your chance," the host said.

Before him was a maze of gigantic proportions, so vast and so intricate, it appeared to go on forever. Always changing and ever the same. Dan asked, "Where are the controls?"

"Right here," the host said, lifting his hands. His voice was as calm and bland as his eyes, which suddenly sharpened into focus. They were eyes that were somehow extremely difficult to look into, yet which called for Dan to look, and delve, and lose himself.

For some reason, perhaps because he thought he heard a voice as beautiful as soft silver chimes, Dan looked away, and started at the sight of the door gradually receding into the distance, moving farther and farther away from him.

The sight scared him so much that he turned from the game. And the eyes.

"You forgot these," the soothing voice said, and somehow the controls were suddenly in his hands. Only they clung to him, like chains trying to drag him into a maze of false desires and lies and deceit which would occupy him with meaningless tasks for all his precious days.

Dan flung the controls at the shadowy host and bolted.

But the soothing voice was still there beside him. "You must be thirsty. Look at this gloriously sparkling pitcher full of ice and lovely water. Won't you stop and drink before you go? What if there is nothing for you outside? What if there is only rock and darkness and cold and fear and thirst and pain? And it is such a long way. Won't you stay here where it is safe? Come, drink with me."

Dan gave no answer. He knew, without being able to explain why, that his only hope lay in a silently total focus on the door.

And just by realizing this, the door was there before him, the knob in his hand. He turned it, and the door opened, and he was through. And he ran.

The janitor kept going on about the dark ages and torture instruments as they pushed and shoved the heavy contraption down the basement corridor, into the elevator, and along the hospital hallway. The wheels had rusted quite a bit in the dank basement, making their progress very slow and extremely noisy. When they passed the nurses' station, Elvira took one look at them and the machine, and her eyes widened to the size of dinner plates. She started to speak, then stopped and popped back out of sight.

Dr. Prain scarcely noticed any of them. He was a driven man.

This machine was the answer to his problem, he knew without question. He would plug it in, heat it up, place the electrode contacts on that Simmons kid's temples, and crank the dial up to the danger level. A couple of red-hot zaps, and that pest would bolt awake. For sure.

Then he, Dr. Prain, would be known as the doctor who had forced the patient to wake up. When the records were transcribed and stowed away, the final notation would be that Dr. Prain was the one who had effected the cure. When that upstart psychiatrist wrote another of his illegible articles, he would be forced to give the credit for the actual cure to Prain and Prain alone. And what was more, the cure would give him the perfect opportunity to repay that galling Simmons kid for some of the hassle he had caused.

Dr. Prain ignored the janitor's continual mutterings and smiled with anticipation as they halted at the patient's door.

The doctor twisted the handle and pushed, but the door did not budge.

He put his shoulder to the door. Harder. Still the door would not open.

"You," Prain barked. "Open this door."

The janitor tried for himself, jiggled the lock, and tried again. Nothing.

"This door is stuck something fierce," he announced. "I better get my tools."

"Well, hurry it up," Dr. Prain snapped, suddenly beset by a ferociously urgent need to get in there and *do* it. When the janitor started walking down the hall, Dr. Prain yelled after him, "Run, man, *run*."

Dan fled into the thickest fog he had ever known. Impenetrable banks of rolling gray mist. He stopped and turned around. Nothing. No door, no lake, no voice. Nothing. There was nothing except mist, which of course was a nothingness all its own.

With the restored power of his inner voice, he cried with the strength of silence for help.

And help came in the form of a wind.

There was a music upon the wind, one heard as much by the heart as by the ears. The music was a lament for things lost.

The wind carried a low bass moaning, a mournful remembrance of all that once had been. Leaves upon unseen trees shivered like tiny silver cymbals, a thousand unshed tears cascading upon the mist. Whispers echoed through the gray, voices from a past when harmony was so constant that nothing else could even be imagined.

The lament called out to him in the eternal language of Spirit. This is what you struggle for, it said. This is a requiem for a time that is past, but borne upon the wind of hope for tomorrow. Go forth, the wind-whispers called in their lilting sibilant tongue. Bring in the new dawn. Become the herald of reborn hope and a promise of peace restored.

Be all that you are intended to be, they sang, a hero for all who are blind, yet yearn for vision that shall witness the end of night.

He turned and saw the mists part to reveal the tower. Faceless, featureless, yet marked with handholds rising up to unseen heights.

He began to climb.

Boom, boom, boom. A great drum within his chest beat time to the song that rang through his being. The relentless beat pressed him onward, driving him to greater determination than he had ever known in his life.

Boom, boom, boom. The sound split the hopeless miasma of fog and guilt and despair as though it did not even exist.

Boom, boom, boom. Life's force rushed in a torrent through his veins, his heart of hearts pounding out the timeless beat of life, of purpose, of hope.

Onward he climbed. Ever onward, ever upward, struggling against the mists of resignation and hopelessness, striving to break through. He clutched onto the very fabric of life and fought on toward the summit.

The storm began just as he grappled up the final rise and flung himself over the ledge. Dan stood, his chest heaving, and looked out over a world gone mad.

Clouds whipped at a frantic pace, swirling in great circles and then being sucked up and away through a vast inverted whirlpool. Lightning flickered and danced in thundering array, great sword fights of fire that split the heavens.

A great wind, not the musical wind that had sung to him below, struck him like a fist. Dan felt his legs being swept from beneath him and took a panic grip upon one leg of an immense iron fire-stand. A second blast of wind stormed upon him full force, and as he was lifted and extended out parallel to the floor, he looked over and saw, lying upon a slab of black stone, the Book of Light. Beyond it, upon another slab, lay a very still, very pale Bliss.

A third blast of wind began working at his grip, and Dan realized that as soon as he was sucked up into the whirlpool, Bliss and the Book would follow in his deadly path.

He opened his mouth and screamed, *"Help!"* But the word was sucked up and swallowed by the wind and the whirlpool toward which all the world was headed.

Yet the call of his heart went forth, its silent strength more powerful than any wind or other earthly force. And it was answered.

A beacon cut through the gloom like a sword of light.

It sliced its way through the storm as though the storm was not even there.

For a moment the darkness faltered, uncertain now of its strength.

Dan lowered himself to stand upon the plateau. He looked out, his vision aided by the new strength that coursed through his frame, and saw a second tower. As he looked, he knew without question that it was the tower that he had climbed with Cousteau and Bliss so long ago. And from the tower there shone a brilliant Light. Dan looked and felt himself drinking in the Light, and knew with the assuredness of gifted wisdom that the Light did not originate there, but was simply being passed from one recipient to another. The Light was a gift.

Cousteau's manor upon the cliffside was raised high, high above the storm and the fury and the surrounding dark, high upon a pinnacle of heavenly power. From its lofty tower there pealed a brilliant illumination, a beacon of hope, a reminder of who he was, and why.

The beacon sought him out, found him, and rested upon him. Dan felt his own strength rekindled by the old man's gift. He raised his arms and felt himself lifted as well—not in body, but in spirit. He knew that no matter what the outcome, he too had come to know the bedrock of truth.

Dan felt his heart surge. He flung his arms upward, as though his heart were too great for his chest, and the only way he could hold himself together was by expanding and releasing and giving forth this love and this light and this confidence and this hope, which poured both from him and from the beacon.

The Light began to stream out from him, weaving together, piercing the darkness, pushing it away, away, farther and farther. The storm faltered yet again, and the whole earth held its breath.

"I bind this land in the name of the Lord of Light," Dan cried, and his cry was given power by his faith and his assurance that he had the right to do so. He lifted his arms higher still and watched as the storm was pushed ever farther back. And though he knew not how, the words were there for him to speak. "I build a wall of thorns around this land and around these people and around this earth, and claim it for all that is good and peaceful. No power shall in times henceforth release this binding and permit the storm to return."

And as he spoke, he saw a wall of Light rise up to the heavens, encircling the valley, higher than the surrounding mountain peaks, loftier than the clouds above.

And he knew that it was so.

"Ah, Dr. Prain! Good, I've been wanting to speak with you," Dr. Meadows said briskly, hustling up.

"Not now, Meadows," Dr. Prain snapped. "I'm busy."

"So am I, but some things can't wait." Dr. Meadows

stepped up, looked down at the apparatus standing beside the door, and said, "Good grief, man! What on earth are you up to?"

"I've had it with that Simmons kid," Dr. Prain said, straightening his stiff-as-a-board white coat.

"That Simmons kid happens to be a patient in this hospital," Dr. Meadows replied angrily.

"Exactly," Dr. Prain said. "And there's no logical reason why he won't wake up. He is a bad influence on the entire hospital. He refuses to respond to treatment. He needs to be corrected." He looked down at the janitor. "How are you doing?"

"Nothing so far," the man replied, leaning back on his haunches and wiping his sweaty brow. "Man, I've seen some doors get stuck in my day, but this one takes the cake."

"Corrected?" Meadows said in exasperation. "Dr. Prain, this is not some street rebel we're discussing here. That Simmons boy is a patient with an unexplained ailment."

"I have discussed the entire matter at length with Dr. Glacey," Dr. Prain replied, his eyes on the janitor's efforts. "He has a new theory."

"That psychiatrist fellow?" Meadows snorted. "Dr. Glacey couldn't thread his shoelaces without coming up with some new theory."

"You are certainly entitled to your opinion," Dr. Prain said stiffly. "However, there are others who think Dr. Glacey's ideas have great merit. Others in positions of authority, I might add. Dr. Glacey has given this patient a careful examination and has concluded that he suffers from post-accident trauma."

"Of all the crazy ideas." Dr. Meadows shook his head. "You two are really clutching at straws, you know that?"

"Dr. Glacey feels that the patient refuses to wake up because he does not wish to face the fear and trauma of his accident," Dr. Prain continued doggedly. "He feels that a good strong shock while he slumbers will force him to leave behind the shelter of sleep."

"So based on this harebrained theory you two have cooked up," Dr. Meadows said, his face growing red, "you're going to go in there and zap the brain of a helpless young man."

Dr. Prain turned around, cocked his head up high, and said down his nose, "That is correct. Unless, of course, you have a better idea."

"I do, as a matter of fact," Dr. Meadows said, keeping a tight grip on his temper. "As the patient continues to wake from time to time, is totally lucid at these points and demonstrates no pain or ill effects whatsoever, I propose that we allow him to sleep until his body has completed whatever healing process it is currently undergoing."

Dr. Prain sniffed contemptuously. "Illogical. Totally illogical. The Simmons patient simply refuses to respond to treatment. If you were to bother to check my records, you would see that for yourself. We have tried everything under our control, and nothing has helped. It is time, Dr. Meadows, for more radical measures."

"You belong in the Middle Ages," Dr. Meadows snapped. "Back when barbers bled their patients to make them well. I bet you'd love that, wouldn't you?"

"If that is all," Dr. Prain said, his nose raised to lofty levels, "I am quite busy."

"No, it is not all," Dr. Meadows said. He gripped Dr. Prain's upper arm and dragged him across the hall and into an empty room.

"What is the meaning of this?"

Dr. Meadows raised up as high as his diminutive frame would allow. "Ruthless logic and a constant desire for control are the two clearest signs I know of limited intelligence."

Dr. Prain drew back as though slapped. "On the contrary, control and orderliness are the only way to maintain a well-functioning hospital."

"The good Lord did not give you a heart for you to try and chain it up inside a tight little box," Dr. Meadows said, thrusting his face within inches of the taller doctor. "Emotions are ours to be used or abused, and brother, yours is the direst case I have ever seen of emotional self-abuse."

"Ah," Dr. Prain said, nodding his head in confident superiority. "It's all clear to me now. You're one of those religious nuts, aren't you?"

But Dr. Meadows wasn't through. "You're just like a modern-day Pharisee, with medicine as your false god. You're so caught up in dotting every 'i' and crossing every 't,' keeping all your little forms in order, you've found what seems to you to be a perfect reason not to care. But let me tell you something, mister. When you stop caring, you stop living."

"You surprise me, doctor," Dr. Prain said coolly. "I thought you were far too intelligent for such nonsense."

"Intelligence is a gift," Dr. Meadows snapped. "Not an excuse for failing to learn how to care. We are here to serve, in case you have forgotten. Serve in this hospital, and serve here on earth. Something you can't do without first learning how to love your fellow man and show compassion for his suffering."

Dr. Prain drew himself up to his full height. "I happen to think that our patients are best served by granting them a functional, orderly, smooth-running hospital. Which requires us to maintain control at all times."

"Aw, baloney." Dr. Meadows stared balefully at the younger doctor. "Well, I can't stop you from practicing medicine, unfortunate as that may be for all your future patients. But sure as God made little green apples, I can stop you from practicing *here*."

"What on earth do you mean by that?"

"You're out, doctor," Dr. Meadows snapped. "Finished, as far as this hospital is concerned. And if I can, I'll make certain you never practice anywhere in this county again."

"The board—"

"On this occasion, the board and I are in perfect agreement. There is to be a special board meeting this afternoon, at which time you may ask for a hearing, if you insist. But why prolong the agony? Consider it done, doctor. You're through." Dr. Meadows watched the younger doctor turn pale. "Now why don't you just wheel that instrument of yours back to the basement where it belongs, and go pack your bags."

–TWENTY–

Dan entered the hospital room as though powering down a long tunnel. The voices came to him first, all stretched out of shape and echoing in a disjointed manner, as though heard through a long tube held to the window of a fast-moving train. Then his swimming vision focused, and he was back.

Really back. Somehow he knew at once that this time his return was for good, and the pain of this knowledge caused him to cry aloud. He looked at the emptiness of his hospital room and saw only what he had lost.

Bliss and Cousteau had been ready to place their gift of thanks upon his head, a slender crown with stars at the peaks. They had been gathered in Cousteau's great room, the Book of Light open upon the table before them, the crown set shimmering upon the pages. Bliss stood beside him, her hands intertwined with his, looking at him with all the feelings of her heart clear in her gaze.

Cousteau had lifted the crown and said in a voice both solemn and proud, "With this crown do we but recognize what has already been granted you from above, Knight Daniel, and offer with it our heartfelt thanks. As you wear it, remember that the crown is not yours. It remains ever the possession of the Lord of Light, as do all gifts, all talents, and all powers granted you. Therefore a part of your daily walk, Knight Daniel, must be the returning of all you are and all you have, including this crown, to the King of all."

Dan had looked down at Bliss, her shining countenance illuminating his heart, with all its dreams and hopes and longings that she had helped awaken in him. He had opened his mouth to tell her how he felt, when suddenly the unseen force had begun drawing him away. Farther and farther, faster and faster, and he could do nothing but cry out at the helplessness and the loss and all that now would never be.

And now this.

Dan could not help but groan again in his pain and despair—for the friends now lost, for the world that for him was no more, and most especially for Bliss. All that was not, all now forever undone and unsaid, all that she was, no more, for him.

Bliss.

The door opened, and a pair of brightly inquisitive eyes popped into view. "Are you all right, son?"

"Hello, Meadows," Dan choked.

Dr. Meadows walked over and looked down on him. "I thought I heard you say something. Are you in pain?"

"It's okay," Dan said. There was nothing the little man could do. "Thanks."

Dr. Meadows took his pulse, listened to his chest, inspected his eyes and ears, then straightened. "Everything appears to be in order," he announced. "I was just in the process of arranging a physical therapist for you. It's high time we started those muscles moving again. If you're going to stick around for a while, I'll go see if she's free."

"There's no rush." Dan sighed.

"Fine. She's Swedish, this lady. Just arrived. Supposed to have some new techniques to show us." Dr. Meadows smiled down at him. "We'll use you as a guinea pig, if that's all right."

Dan nodded, his thoughts and heart elsewhere.

He was left alone for a time, but as there was nothing but loss to keep him company, he did not mark time's passage. Then there was a soft knock at the door, and he heard a voice as beautiful as soft silver chimes say, "May I come in, please?"

Dan bolted upright.

The door pushed opened further to reveal a young woman with hair the color of sun-ripened wheat and eyes of cornflower blue. Around her neck was a bit of gold, which caught the light and sent it shimmering back into his eyes and heart.

He cried, "Bliss!"

She took a frightened step back. "How can you know my name?"

"I understand," he cried. "I wasn't ready to meet you before. But now I am! I've learned the lesson!"

Her pretty forehead creased, then lightened. "Ah, I understand. The good Dr. Meadows, he told you to tease with me because I am new, yes?"

Dan leaned back, content. "Yes," he agreed quietly.

"Then perhaps we can stop with the joking and begin—" Bliss stopped and peered at his side table. "Did you perhaps forget to turn off a light?"

"What?"

She pointed. "There is something glowing in your drawer. May I?" She walked over, opened the drawer, and gasped.

Upon the Book there rested a slender golden crown.

–Twenty-one–

When the knock came at the door, Consuela assumed the social worker had decided to stop by again. She was pretty much the only visitor they had.

The caseworker woman was coming by more often these days. Consuela wondered if perhaps she felt guilty about Consuela having had to stay so long in the hospital. As though the woman had had anything to do with it.

The knock sounded again. Consuela walked slowly through the dingy apartment. Her spark for life had dwindled in the weeks since leaving the hospital. The door to Cousteau and Napoleon and the others had closed for good, it seemed. This left her trapped in a world where she knew she did not belong.

She opened the apartment door. Her eyes widened until they almost popped from her head. "Daniel!"

"You're a hard person to find," he said, handing her an enormous bouquet.

"Flowers!" Consuela had difficulty seeing around them. "Are these for me?"

"My mom always told me that a gentleman takes flowers when visiting the home of a lady," he said.

Then Consuela caught sight of what nestled in the crook of his other arm. "Napoleon!"

"He can't talk yet," Dan said. "But I'm working on that."

Dan took a step to one side, revealing what had remained hidden behind him.

Consuela's squeal rose another octave. "Bliss!"

"Put those flowers in water, grab your coat, and let's move," Dan told her.

"Where are we going?"

"I've found Cousteau," Dan replied. "He's invited us over. He says he'll teach us about the Book."